DOUBLE MURDER AT THE GRAND HOTEL MIRAMARE

Elena & Michela Martignoni

Originally Published as *Doppio delitto al Miramare*

Kazabo Publishing

MAIN CHARACTERS

Luigi Berté	Deputy Assistant Chief of Police
Pasquale Parodi	Berté's Sergeant
Mariella Gianasio	Detective, Genoa Homicide Unit
Roberto Terani	Genoa Chief of Police
Enzo Grossi	Chiavari District Attorney
Francesca Belli	Police Officer
Fausto Sabatini	Police Officer
Lucio Franchini	Medical Examiner
Marzia Penza	Berté's Landlady
Patty Astesani	Berté's girlfriend in Milan
Countess Licia Van Der Meer	Guest at the Grand Hotel Miramare
Roberto Sommariva	Countess Van Der Meer's accountant
Alessia Sommariva	Roberto Sommariva's daughter
Ornella Ferrari	Countess Van Der Meer's secretary
Gianna Ferrari	Countess Van Der Meer's ex-secretary
Claudia Ferrari	Ornella Ferrari's sister
Antonio Brioschi	Ornella Ferrari's ex-boyfriend
Elio Garaventa	Manager of the Grand Hotel Miramare
Pablo Polledo	Guest of the Grand Hotel Miramare
Colonel Badeschi	Guest of the Grand Hotel Miramare

Commendator
Olindo De Cillis   Guest of the Grand Hotel Miramare

Fernando Luis Gomez Guest of the Grand Hotel Miramare

Dario Dalmasso   De Cillis's caregiver

Pierluigi Frilli   Bartender at the Grand Hotel Miramare

Consuelo   Maid at the Grand Hotel Miramare

FACT OR FICTION?

Double Murder at the Grand Hotel Miramare is a work of fiction, but the place where the story is set is very real. The sleepy village of Lungariva is, in fact, the village of Santa Margherita Ligure, on the Italian Riviera, and all the places, shops and restaurants mentioned in the book are real places in and around Santa Margherita Ligure.

Even the Grand Hotel Miramare is a real place, a historic luxury Liberty-style hotel overlooking the Gulf of Tigullio in Santa Margherita Ligure. The Grand Hotel Miramare opened its doors in 1903 and glided serenely through the 20th century with all its charm and allure intact. Well-known for exemplary service and outstanding cuisine, it became a magnet for international high society the day it opened and continues to draw the well-heeled – and the well-informed – even today. The hotel has welcomed guests like Sir Laurence Olivier and Vivian Leigh, who spent their honeymoon there, King Hussein of Jordan, King Constantine of Greece, Prince Rainier and Princess Grace of Monaco, and Sophia Loren. But perhaps the hotel's most extraordinary guest was Guglielmo Marconi who transmitted the first radiotelegraphy and radiotelephony signals in history from the hotel terrace in 1933.

TABLE OF CONTENTS

PREFACE

Deputy Assistant Chief of Police Luigi Berté, having just left the police station after an exhausting day's work, decided to take a walk along the boardwalk to relax. Unfortunately, instead of relaxing, he suffered a sudden pang of discontent. After the trouble he stirred up in Milan and the forced transfer to Lungariva, he was falling into these bad moods alarmingly often… And his conscience, that little voice that never missed an opportunity to taunt him, was always lying in wait with a snotty comment. Even now he heard it say,

Too late for remorse!

But what remorse? Thinking back on it, he felt like an idiot. He could have acted differently, with more tact or wit… but the fact remained that if the occasion were to present itself again, he would behave in the same way. And so they transferred him, from Milan to a sleepy town on the Ligurian coast. Here in Lungariva, everybody knew about his "punitive" transfer, and everyone had an opinion on it. But regardless, they had to deal with a cranky, unhappy, and irritable forty-year-old deputy assistant chief who kept his hair long and tied in a messy ponytail.

'But do I care about what my colleagues think? Not a bit! Let them deal with it!' thought Berté shrugging his shoulders, trying to shake off both the tension built up throughout the day and the bad mood he suddenly found himself in.

Another lie!

His conscience – usually referred to by Berté as "the Bastard" – interrupted again, with no consideration at all. Luckily, by this point he was used to it. Luigi Berté sat down on a bench opposite the beach and rubbed his hand across his forehead. The humidity of the small Ligurian town was aggravating his migraines, making him long for Milan, the city where he was born and raised. His parents, however, were from the South and so he often felt torn between two places and cultures. He wasn't northern or southern, but something in between. His punctuality was definitely Milanese, but his jealousy, thoroughly tested by his sort-of-ex-girlfriend, Patty… was certainly southern. Even physically, Berté was a contradiction, with the dark skin and charcoal eyes typical of southern Italy, and the height of a Dane.

And where did the extra pounds come from?

'And there you go again, you Bastard. I knew you were going to ask that,' thought Berté, annoyed. But the jab at his extra pounds suddenly reminded him that at the boarding house, the *pensione,* where he was staying (while waiting to find more permanent lodgings), an excellent dinner awaited him… skillfully cooked by the charming and plump landlady with whom he had recently begun a relationship. At the thought of Marzia awaiting him with her bright smile and that patience and positivity which he had fallen in love with, his bad mood started to dissipate… and even the migraine that had started to creep in seemed to back off. Perhaps the exile to Lungariva was not so bad after all.

The First Day

Lungariva, a morning in late March

Different, yet all the same. Different faces, bodies, ages. Different means, places, weapons. The same motives: money, revenge, jealousy, insanity…

And above all, the same terrible anger that gripped him whenever he found himself face-to-face with a new murder victim.

Anger that brings trouble.

'Yes, you Bastard, precisely that.' This is what Deputy Assistant Chief Luigi Berté was thinking as he surveyed two corpses riddled by a still unknown number of bullets.

It was Easter Monday – Saint Angel's day, as they call it in Italy – and fifteen minutes earlier he had been strolling along Lungariva's waterfront. Bright sun reflected from the waves though the air still carried a touch of winter crispness. With his hands in his pockets, his conspicuous, frizzy and graying ponytail popping out of the collar of his black coat, and his ear buds in, he listened to the deep voice of one of his favorite singer-songwriters, Claudio Sanfilippo. The song "Pandora" was narrating a sailboat's journey in the wind, a sailboat just like those Berté was now watching glide over the sea, with their proud bows and their swaying masts.

Easter marked the true start of Lungariva's tourist season. Row boats – called *gozzi* in Liguria – sailboats, and motorboats were being prepared for the summer that loomed just around the corner. The beaches were being cleared of all the flotsam and jetsam – which, if Berté was honest, was mostly unromantic trash – washed ashore during the winter. Houses all along the waterfront were getting their spring cleanings, ready to host the vacationers who were about to throng the small town. In short, there was a lot of activity, even a small invasion of rowdy tourists, sprawled out under the sun to catch the first tan of the season, or bustling between shops, cafés and restaurants.

Berté preferred the deserted and sleepy Lungariva of the fall and winter.

Fifteen minutes earlier he had thought, 'Here I am again in my Ligurian prison... a single man walking along the nearly deserted harbor...'

Just off the coast a large ship passed by, heading toward an unknown destination. Maybe its destination was the Atlantic or the East, who knows...

Marzia's husband would soon board a similar ship. Captain Marco Pestarino, a real *cornuto* – the Italian expression for a man with an unfaithful wife – with a know-it-all air about him, married to the woman Berté considered "his."

A woman you have no right to.

Fifteen minutes earlier, Berté remembered it well, he had hoped the captain would make some mistake and disappear at sea for a couple of months. With Pestarino around, nothing substantial had happened between him and Marzia. Glances, secret kisses in the hallways of the boarding house, the need to talk and hold one another, all communicated through small gestures and hundreds of texts.

Two conspirators.

Indeed. Since returning from Milan, however, he was determined to sort out their relationship once and for all. It had started almost like a game, out of curiosity and to drive away the loneliness, but it had became important, at least to him.

Fifteen minutes earlier he was watching the yachts bobbing in the port with a touch of envy before turning his eyes to the green hills, dotted with houses, that closed off the gulf.

He could already taste the lunch that would be waiting for him at the Pensione Aurora. That morning Marzia had approached him describing the day's menu. Something light, she specified, to help him watch his weight: a small appetizer of vegetables and *panissa*, a traditional Genoese fried chickpea finger food; spelt fettuccine sautéed in pesto sauce with a long list of vegetables flavored with extra-virgin olive oil followed by vegetable ravioli with raw butter, marjoram and flakes of parmesan; lamb chops with herbs and baked potatoes or crusted salmon; *Colomba*, a dove-shaped Easter cake, with mascarpone cream, and to finish a grapefruit sorbet and chocolate eggs, followed by coffee and the ever-present limoncello.

Ooh. Quite the health nut, aren't you, Berté?

Berté swallowed like he had already tasted everything.

After all, he was learning not to care so much about his figure.

Lies.

His conscience was right. When he looked at himself in the mirror, he would suck his stomach in. Two-hundred three pounds was the last reading on the scale.

'But I do have a thin face,' he said to himself.

Hooray. The only thin part of you… better than nothing, I suppose!

No one would mistake Marzia for a swimsuit model, but he found her fantastic just for that reason. He loved her curves. And her face… her face was beautiful, a Madonna by Raphael.

And she's married to George Clooney.

'Let's not exaggerate!' Berté thought. 'Pestarino is handsome enough, but taking a closer look at him…'

And only fifteen minutes earlier, while he had been enumerating Pestarino's defects to himself and perversely enjoying it, he had received the call from Sergeant Parodi.

A double murder has a way of distracting you from your thoughts, as well as ruining your plans. As he hung up, Berté had looked up towards the hotel where the murder had taken place.

He had seen the blue sign with the hotel's name on the roof many times before. An ordinary name, Miramare: Sea view. You can find a Grand Hotel Miramare in every small seaside town, but what had just happened there certainly wasn't ordinary.

After a few minutes walk, Berté found himself in front of the impressive baroque building overlooking the sea, surrounded by a very well-kept garden with a large swimming pool, still empty after the winter. On the hotel's bright white façade, there were open shutters painted in an intense sky blue. Some floral wreaths decorated the upper part of the building, while an Italian flag, fixed to a staff, waved above the sign reading: MIRAMARE. Berté crossed the street, glancing at the still empty beach below, and climbed the double staircase that led to the entrance covered in glass and gold. Sergeant Parodi was waiting for him in the lobby and together they went up to the fourth floor and entered room 422. There he found the two bodies whose stolen lives would consume his in the days to come.

The man was lying on his back. He looked around sixty, but could have been older. Graying hair, regular features, a light tan. Apart from the face, only his muscular arms were visible; the rest of the body was covered with a sheet and bedspread pierced by at least four bullet holes. Another shot, probably the fatal one, had struck him in the temple.

It didn't seem like the work of a professional, Berté mused, but given the number of rounds fired at random, something very personal. The killer's enthusiasm suggested both little familiarity with weapons and blind rage. The shots had probably been fired from about ten feet away, judging by the casings on the floor. Berté could see a few of them near the door. But that wasn't definitive. They could have rolled or been accidentally disturbed by whoever had fled the room after discovering the murder. He bent over to inspect them. They were 9mm casings. He also looked under the bed and saw that the pistol was there. It often happened that the weapon was abandoned at the scene, especially when the serial number had been filed off. From what he could see, and by the type of the casings, it was a semi-automatic with a silencer, a Beretta 98 to be exact: the civilian version of the 9mm Beretta 92 FS Parabellum used by the Armed Forces and the police. The fact that it had a silencer attached confirmed that it had been acquired illegally. A rather average pistol, with a 15-round magazine, in this case empty, given that the breech was open. The ballistic analysis and forensic findings would either confirm or deny his hypothesis that this was the murder weapon.

Berté stood back up and approached the other side of the bed, where the woman was lying. Estimated age: about forty. She was face down, with no clothes. Her blond hair, crusted with dried blood, was strewn over the pillow. A shot had partially destroyed the back of her head. She had also been wounded in her back and legs. A looker, from what was visible.

Suddenly, for no good reason, Berté found himself fantasizing. The plot for a story erupted – that was the right word – in his mind.

Right now? Really?

Yes, his conscience was right, this wasn't the time for playing writer, but he knew that as soon as he had a spare moment, he would shut himself in his room and sit at his desk in front of the computer. His sudden, barely-suppressed anger triggered his imagination but his passion for writing was a secret he kept well safeguarded.

He was exchanging a few words with the paramedics who had been first on the scene in answer to the 911 call when he realized that Parodi was whispering something to him.

"Sir, the manager of the hotel is outside the door. I told him not to come in so as to not contaminate the crime scene."

Berté nodded. Pasquale Parodi was the ideal sergeant: precise, attentive to the rules, a man of few words.

The manager, a tall man, skinny, blond, and with pale eyes, stood in the doorway. He looked like he was in his fifties and was wearing an elegant gray suit with a dark tie. Berté suspected it had an expensive label. He had been educated on how to recognize prestigious brands by fashion enthusiast Patty, his ex-girlfriend. Berté suspected the manager was normally a smooth operator. Certainly, he was used to dealing with a high profile clientele. But under the circumstances, even the most accomplished professionalism might have broken down, thought Berté, noticing a layer of sweat on the manager's balding forehead. He met him at the door and shook his hand.

"Deputy Assistant Chief Berté."

"Elio Garaventa, nice to meet you," responded the manager, holding out his right hand. "I'm shocked. In my ten years as manager nothing has ever happened like this before. Some natural deaths yes, this time however... I don't know how the clients will react." The manager's voice trembled.

"We'll try not to be difficult, but we have to do our job and we can't always be discrete..."

Honestly, almost never.

"The first hours are critical, so prepare yourself: Soon, like they say in the movies, all hell is going to break loose."

"I imagined as much. I thought I'd reserve a room for you for the investigation... You know, Sir, I would like to try to separate the guests from..." The manager was struggling to stay detached.

"From us?" Berté came to his aid. "Thank you. A room will be useful. I think we'll stay here for the forensic examinations, at least today and tomorrow."

"And the press?" Garaventa asked with obvious concern.

Berté laid his hand on the manager's shoulder in an attempt to comfort him.

"In a couple of minutes, they'll swarm the hotel. You frequently host important conferences, so you must be used to journalists. We'll do our best to keep them out of your hair, but it won't be easy. The ones on the crime beat are the most stubborn, they'll always be after you and they never back down."

The manager nodded, increasingly distraught.

"Who are the victims?" asked Berté.

"Two permanent guests of the hotel: Signor Roberto Sommariva and Signorina Ornella Ferrari, accountant and secretary of Countess Van Der Meer. The countess is one of our most important clients. Signor Sommariva arrived three years ago with the countess. Signorina Ferrari, on the other hand, has only been here for six months, that is to say since the previous secretary retired."

"Are they married? To each other I mean."

"No, no… only, let's say, colleagues. They both have private rooms in the hotel. This suite is Signor Sommariva's. He was using it as an office, whereas Signorina Ornella was on the floor below."

Berté noticed a trace of embarrassment in the manager's eyes.

There was some sort of connection here. But what it was not altogether clear. His gaze jumped to a small table where there sat a silver ice bucket with the neck of a champagne bottle peeking out. At least they'd had a nice drink before their untimely demise.

"Lovers, then?"

Garaventa shook his head.

"I don't know, Inspector, certainly, the circumstances suggest…" he broke off, making it clear that he would not say anything else for the time being. Indeed, it was too early to delve into the subject.

Berté nodded hello to Francesca Belli and Fausto Sabatini, the two young rookie officers from the Lungariva police station.

"Who found them?" he asked the manager.

"Consuelo, one of the maids. The countess sent her to look for them. At nine o'clock they always had breakfast together, but this morning neither of the two answered their cell phone or their room phone. After knocking on the door at both of their rooms and getting no response, the girl came to get me and I opened the door with the master key… I turned on the light and…! Who could have done such a thing? How is it possible that no one heard anything, not even a scream?" The manager rubbed a hand across his face.

"I believe the victims didn't have time to scream," responded Berté. "They were sleeping, and the murderer had a pistol with a silencer."

The director put a hand over his eyes exclaiming, "Terrible! Killed in their sleep!"

"Can you confirm that the room was locked when this Consuelo checked?" asked Berté.

"Yes, yes, locked and with no sign of a break-in. I should tell you that yesterday a maid reported a missing master key. She had left it in the office last night when she went to dinner. When she went to look for it this morning, she realized that it wasn't there anymore…" The manager left the sentence unfinished, staring at Berté with dismay.

"We must speak with this maid immediately," said Berté, signaling to Belli who nodded. "You both entered the room. Did you touch anything? Step on any bullet casings by chance?" continued Berté.

"No, no… we didn't touch anything and we didn't even get near the bodies."

"And what's behind that?" Berté pointed at a door.

"The bathroom and another room. Signor Sommariva and the countess were using it as an office."

"Sabatini, Belli, check and make sure they're empty." ordered Berté, speaking to his colleagues.

"Maybe the murderer was searching for something, perhaps some documents. What does she do for a living? I mean, the… what did you say her name is?" he asked, leaving the room with the manager.

"Countess Licia Trevisan, widow of Count Van Der Meer. The countess has an enormous estate to manage. Mines and land in South Africa, inherited from her husband."

Garaventa looked away, making it clear that he did not want to go into specifics. That suited Berté. But he would return to it later.

"Notify the victim's relatives," Berté ordered Parodi.

"Poor Signora Gianna…" said the manager dejectedly.

"Who's Signora Gianna?"

"The countess's ex-secretary. She's also Signorina Ornella's aunt. Six months ago she gave up her position and let her niece take over because of health problems."

"Listen, I have a lot of things to ask you and I expect your total cooperation. The sooner we catch the killer, the sooner we'll be out of your hotel. My men will be asking you a series of questions and will have several requests for you. I'll be sending for you later myself."

"Perhaps you'd care to have lunch with me, Inspector..." Garaventa proposed.

"Yes, great idea. I'd ask that you provide Sergeant Parodi with a list of employees, even those that weren't working over the last few days. And tell him the story about the missing master key... Oh, and it's important to know who has left the hotel since last evening. Did any guests leave before you discovered the murder?"

Garaventa shook his head decisively.

"No, nobody."

"And did any guests check out today?"

The manager hesitated briefly. "I don't think so, but I'll go check. It's possible, however, that someone will want to leave now... given the circumstances."

"Don't let anyone leave without telling us. We can't hold your guests here, but we at least need to know who they are in case we need a statement before they go."

The manager gave a sharp nod and walked away followed by Parodi.

Berté went back into the room dreading the mountain of work that awaited him. An unforgettable Easter Monday.

"Sir," said officer Belli, "it's all clear in there. There's quite a lot of accounting books, two laptops, a printer. It's a real office."

"Remember, guys: eyes and ears open. Warn your families that they won't see you for a little while and... let the games begin! We are going to have our work cut out for us with this one."

He looked at the couch where a woman's purse rested and at the nightstand that held a mobile phone.

"Sabatini, you check the secondary entrances and any other possible ways to enter the hotel. You, Belli, stay here in front of the door until forensics arrives. Don't let anybody in."

The whirlwind of tasks to do and statements to take continued to grow in Berté's head. If he let confusion reign, the case would become a tower of Babel that would collapse on him – and his career. A double murder in a completely packed hotel the night between Easter Sunday and Monday seemed straight out of a novel, but unfortunately, it was all too real.

He went out into the hallway and dialed his superior. Terani picked up after two rings. The chief of police's natural kindness could put anyone he spoke to in a good mood. Berté loved him because he was the only person who had never asked him, either directly or indirectly, to cut his ponytail. He knew that an official representative of law and order probably shouldn't look like an ageing rock star. So far, his reputation as a detective had stifled any complaints, however.

Berté reported the facts to his superior. The chief of police was silent for a moment, then assigned the case to him, adding, however, that he would be working side-by-side with a homicide unit and a forensics team from Genoa.

It wasn't ideal to have to collaborate with people that he didn't know, but, considering that there were almost two hundred people to interview, he couldn't do it quickly enough with just his officers from Lungariva. The prosecutor would surely want the witness statements as soon as possible, so he'd need help. He thanked his superior who finished with some additional instructions before ending the call with a 'keep me informed and don't argue with your colleagues.'

Now he had to notify the prosecutor on call. Berté expected him to be in a bad mood, given that it was a holiday, but Grossi said that he would be there right away from Chiavari without batting an eye. In fact, he seemed almost glad to be called away.

Festive family lunches aren't always as nice as you might hope.

I would have liked to have one, snorted Berté to himself, saying goodbye to Marzia's menu… But after all, she was not 'his family' and until Pestarino set sail for South America, finally leaving them free, Marzia was off limits.

He dialed the number of the Pensione Aurora. A velvety voice filled his ears, evoking the usual emotion.

"Pensione Aurora, hello, this is Marzia."

"Um… it's me."

"Luigi, when are you coming?"

"Unfortunately, I'm not coming… there was a double murder at the Grand Hotel."

"What? You're kidding me!" Marzia fell silent for a second, "Listen, don't waste your time with me. Let's do this: I'll put something aside for you in case you can stop by later. Go now..." her voice became a whisper, "kisses."

Berté stood there like a fool with his phone in hand while a shiver went down his spine. Marzia always managed to surprise him.

If you're quite finished, it might be a good time to get your ample butt in gear!

This time, the Bastard was correct. This was not the moment to be thinking about his personal life.

A sudden, intense fragrance made him turn.

He put the phone in his pocket and approached the door leading into the room where the murder took place. A woman was talking with Belli in the doorway. About seventy-five, tall, blond – impeccably blond – thin and elegant. She was wearing a bright blue pantsuit over a milky white blouse. Pearl earrings, pearl necklace, pearl bracelets. And eyes of an intense blue, almost periwinkle, with a powder blue eye shadow that brought out their brilliance.

Someone you would call a great old lady, if there wasn't always a hint of disrespect in the phrase 'old lady.' She must have been a woman of rare beauty, when she was young...

Great consolation.

Yeah, who cares how you used to be? How you are today is what matters to people. You're judged for that, not for the past...

And enough with the philosophy!

As Berté approached, the woman looked him up and down with suspicion.

"Deputy Assistant Chief Berté," he anticipated, showing her his card. "You are..."

"Countess Licia Van Der Meer."

Her voice was piercing, clear, very crisp. There was a slightly odd inflection, but Berté couldn't figure out which language the accent came from.

"This is a crime scene, ma'am, you can't enter," he said, overwhelmed by her perfume. "But if you want to look..." he said, opening the door and turning on the light. He feigned indifference, but scrutinized her reaction.

Van Der Meer stared at the bodies. Berté saw terror and fear and also a hint of pain, all well disguised, however, under a fake indifference. She lingered for a few seconds on the bodies, then her eyes, in which Berté thought he could detect a hint of tears, fell on him. Her gaze had a magnetism he found difficult to resist.

"Were they your employees?" he asked, pointing at the victims.

"Yes." The woman's tone hardened as if it troubled her that those two mangled bodies had had anything to do with her life.

"I'll have a lot of questions to ask you, ma'am."

Deputy Assistant Chief Robespierre doesn't give a damn about titles of nobility.

Of course he doesn't! Ever since he had studied the French Revolution, he hated noble pleasantries. He would never give that woman the satisfaction of calling her *countess.*

"I have some procedures to…" But he didn't finish the sentence because Van Der Meer turned her back to him and walked away down the hallway, trembling and sobbing.

As quick as the leopard whose fur coat she probably has in her closet.

Berté's anger at this aristocratic insolence dissipated harmlessly because Franzini, the medical examiner, had just entered the room.

"And forensics?" asked the irritated doctor, without greeting Berté.

"They're coming from Genoa. Chief's orders," responded Berté.

The coroner grumbled. Without the forensics team he couldn't begin his examination. He groaned an 'even during the holidays!' – a sentiment with which Berté was in perfect agreement – and shook his head.

"Dearest Berté, why is it that since the day you started working here in Lungariva, I haven't had a moment's peace?"

"Are you suggesting I'm responsible for this mess?"

"You said it, not me." snickered the coroner. "You would think people would be a little more considerate and refrain from committing murders on three-day weekends. Anyway, while we wait, I would guess that the time of death would be one, at the latest two in the morning. Based on my keen eye and years of experience, I suspect we will find that the cause of death in both cases was gunshot wounds. Of course, only the autopsy will plumb the depths of these mysterious deaths and reveal the hidden truth."

"It could be the sacred Easter holiday, but you seem more poetic than usual."

In response, the coroner favored him with an intricate curse in the Genoese dialect that Berté couldn't decipher.

"Poetic? Certainly not!" exclaimed Franzini, opening his bag. "I was off to go see my brother in La Spezia and enjoy some excellent fish. Instead…"

"Well, I'll try and see to it that you don't miss your meal. And while you're enjoying your fish, I'll be stuck here, and in it up to my neck."

"Tough job. When is this forensics team coming?"

"Give them time. With the Easter Monday traffic it will take more than half an hour from Genoa…"

"Was it really necessary for them to come from the city?" asked the doctor with disdain. Berté sighed, opening his arms wide.

"We're going to need reinforcements. It's not going to be an easy case."

"I suppose not," confirmed Franzini, cleaning his glasses with a cloth, "but it's going to be a real pain in the ass for you to have them here."

"They'll come in handy, you'll see," remarked Berté, internally rolling his eyes at his own smarminess.

"If you say so…" The coroner wandered off to further examine the bodies.

"Parodi!" roared Berté, wondering where he had gone.

"Here, Sir!" responded the sergeant entering with Grossi, the prosecutor. The prosecutor, a middle aged man – not very tall, a bit chubby, with an honest face and thick reading glasses – surveyed the room before shaking the hand that Berté extended to him and greeting the coroner with a nod.

"A fine mess…" he said, diverting his gaze from the bodies indicating with his head that they should leave the room. "You're definitely going to need some backup."

Berté felt the word "backup" increasingly irking him, like a constant itch. He was also aware that it wouldn't go away any time soon.

"The chief of police already assigned me a homicide team from Genoa," he said, trying to sound extremely pleased. "They're coming with the forensics team."

Grossi nodded, muttering a "good, good" and smiling apathetically.

"Listen to me, Berté, please don't start arguing with everyone…"
Your reputation precedes you.

"No problem, Sir, I'm used to collaborating..." Berté reassured the prosecutor, leaving the sentence unfinished. He would have liked to add "even with assholes," but restrained himself.

"How about a coffee, Sir?" he offered in an effort to change the subject.

"Yes, please. You'll join me, right? I have some things to discuss with you privately."

"Parodi!" Berté called again. "The manager promised me a private room..."

"Yes, yes, follow me, Sir," the sergeant interrupted. "Signor Garaventa reserved us a private area we can use as an incident room for the investigation. Belli and Sabatini will keep an eye on the crime scene and wait for the team from Genoa. I'll have your coffees sent up."

Berté put a hand on his shoulder to thank him.

While getting in the elevator his phone rang. When he saw 'Patty' appear on the screen, Berté was tempted not to answer, but knowing his ex's stubbornness, and fearing being called every fifteen minutes for the rest of the day, he decided to get it over with and tapped the green button.

"Hi, Patty, how are you?" he asked in a low voice.

"Like yesterday, when I wished you a happy Easter, you old grouch!"

"I'm happy for you... Me, on the other hand..."

But Patty, as usual, was not listening to him and interrupted.

"Listen, Luigi, why don't I come to Lungariva for a few days, I'm on vacation and..."

"Ah no! No, no, absolutely not!" shouted Berté. The prosecutor stared at him.

"You pig! Don't yell!" squealed Patty.

"Patty," said Berté trying to calm his voice. "I'm in the middle of a complicated investigation, I wouldn't even have time to say hello, much less spend any time with you. Let's do it another time."

"Investigations, investigations... Even on Easter! Always the same old story! The same old bullsh..."

"Well fuck you!" exploded Berté. "Read the paper tomorrow! Ciao!"

He hung up the phone, but not quickly enough: Patty's string of inventive profanities filled the confined space.

Speaking of nobility...

"I'm sorry, Sir, but..." Berté spread his arms feeling the need to explain.

"Don't apologize," Grossi smiled, "you should have heard what my wife said this morning when I came out on this case. Not to mention her mother and my three daughters!"

It sounded like the prosecutor had had a lucky escape, thought Berté, entering what Sergeant Parodi had indicated was to be their new incident room. Normally, it must have been used for conferences or work lunches, or perhaps weddings. It had the usual elegance of a luxury hotel, and large windows and a French door leading into the garden.

"Where do we start?" asked Grossi, now in full prosecutor mode, as he sat down at a table. Berté summarized what he had already discovered about the two victims and the pistol.

"Could the weapon tell us something?" asked Grossi.

"Hopefully there are some fingerprints, but I doubt it. We'll see what the forensics team says. I want to post several people in the hotel – quite a lot of people come through here. There are well over a hundred guests and about forty staff members. As soon as I go through the lists, I'll pass them along, but we can't rule out the possibility that the murderer came from outside, committed the act, and left. If not, the killer is probably still in the hotel."

"Ok," Grossi nodded, "I suggest we do an initial screening. After the statements I'll meet with anyone you think is suspicious. The countess will be the first one to question, both victims worked for her, no? So she'll have the most information. We have to find out if someone made good on a threat or if those two were involved in something dishonest. Examine the accountant's files carefully. You told me that the countess is a wealthy woman so there could be blackmail, corruption, or revenge..."

Berté nodded, remembering the lady with the blue eyes. "We also have a report of a lost master key," he said, "a maid claims that she lost it and given that there weren't any signs of a break-in..."

"The murderer could have stolen the master key and entered the room..." the prosecutor sighed and then started again. "Have you notified the families of the victims?"

Berté nodded. "I need authorization to check the cell phones. I already asked the hotel reception to hand over their phone records. I want printouts of all of the phone calls from the last week along with the booking emails. Then there are the computer files, but before examining those I'll need to make a forensic copy."

"Do you think we need an expert?" asked the prosecutor.

"No, for now I think the forensics team from Genoa will be enough. If not, we'll bring in an outside consultant."

The prosecutor confirmed Berté's plans with a sharp nod and sat pondering for a few moments. Perhaps he, too, was thinking about the immense amount of work that needed to be organized, and how it was still too soon to rely on gut feeling.

"How should I deal with guests that want to leave the hotel?" Berté asked him. "Some might prefer to leave right away and we can't keep them here."

Grossi adjusted his glasses on his nose and took out some files from the leather briefcase he had placed at his feet. "Question them right away and if they haven't got anything interesting to say, let them go, otherwise send them to me. We can't have over a hundred suspects. We'll need to use our instincts and discretion. Ah, here's the coffee."

A waiter, or rather a barista, given the black apron he wore on his waist, carried in a tray and china that would have done credit to Buckingham Palace. Berté and the prosecutor were impressed by the elegance and the wide variety of pastries and confections that were included.

"Special treatment," whispered Grossi, winking at Berté.

Parodi caught them in mid-feast and eating delicate cookies and chocolate eggs. To make matters worse, the sergeant wasn't alone. He was accompanied by a group of officers, following a young woman in plainclothes.

Berté found himself shaking hands and making introductions with a mouthful of crumbs. Shameful.

So much for first impressions.

"Detective Gianasio!" exclaimed the prosecutor, shaking the woman's hand with enthusiasm. "I'm pleased the police chief sent you."

The young woman had an honest face, large dark green eyes, and wavy blond hair. Tall and skinny, Detective Mariella Gianasio had the grace and elegance of a model.

"I would like to introduce you to Deputy Assistant Chief Berté, who will coordinate the investigation," the prosecutor said.

Detective Gianasio looked at Berté with surprise and shook his hand vigorously.

"I've heard of you!" she exclaimed with a strong accent from Bergamo, a Northern city near Milan. She looked curiously at his ponytail. Berté wasn't sure if it was in admiration or disapproval.

"Our Berté is already famous in Tigullio," the prosecutor interjected.

Berté responded with a polite little laugh.

Lame.

"So let's get to work," Grossi ordered, "Forensics, upstairs!"

Detective Gianasio nodded and three of her officers set off behind Parodi.

"As for the others, I would like you all to work on the witness statements because there are so many of them," continued the prosecutor. "Berté, you and your men handle the hotel guests, and you, Gianasio, the hotel staff."

After arranging a few more formalities and some necessary paperwork, the prosecutor left, saying he would rejoin them sometime in the afternoon.

"Okay Sir, I'll get started," Gianasio nodded to Berté as she rose from her seat.

"You're not Ligurian…" Berté said, unable to stop himself.

"No, I'm from Bergamo and I can't hide it, even though I've lived in Genoa for three years. You're not exactly a local either!" she snorted.

"Correct. My mother was from Calabria and my father was from Lombardy." Berté admitted, standing up in turn. Gianasio gave him an eloquent look and made her way to the door.

Left alone, Berté began to leaf through the list of guests that Sabatini had printed for him, knowing Berté preferred to read on paper rather than on a screen. Families, for the most part, many of them foreigners, for a total of one hundred and two people, of which thirty were children.

There were, in addition, fifteen elderly people, with and without caregivers. They couldn't be ruled out beforehand, but it was unlikely that one of them was the killer. Five of them had been residing at the Grand Hotel for more than a month. The single rooms were occupied by a South American businessman, two middle-aged German women with a friend of theirs from Florence, and three Russians in their fifties.

What a cast of suspects! It was like something in a classic detective novel, except instead of a dozen people locked in a country house, he had to sort through a hundred people, any of whom could disappear on the next train. He remembered a book he had read during the summer and enjoyed very much... but the title? He could picture Necchi, the bookseller with a red beret and bowtie, saying, "You can't miss it, it was written by Augusto De Angelis... He's considered the father of Italian crime novels and all of his books are really good." Necchi knew more about books than the Devil... but what was it called? He remembered it very well. It didn't involve a hotel but it had a long list of suspects and a very well-crafted plot in which everyone had hidden motivations. And everything came together in a very satisfying conclusion.

You should be so lucky with this case!

Was it possible that he could not recall the title? He could even picture the book sitting on the shelf of his library back in Milan! He knew this was going be like a splinter lodged in the back of his mind until he remembered.

The arrival of the waiter, who invited him to have lunch with the manager, interrupted his reverie. He sighed. One o'clock already, he thought, following the waiter, and he still hadn't gotten anything done. He was a man of action, but in a case like this, actions had to be meticulously planned and coordinated, otherwise you'd have chaos and disaster. Berté wanted to capture the murderer immediately and drag him into court so he could receive the punishment he deserved. This was the way things were supposed to work, in life as in literature. Instead, just the week before, he had read a thriller, written by a district attorney, which had disappointed him: the policeman, once he discovered the killer, decided to obscure the facts and destroy the evidence because he sympathized with the guilty party.

No! He had never have done that, would never do that. And in

Milan he had proved it!

Risking your job…

Blame it on Grandma Peppa's DNA. That woman respected life to the point that she wouldn't even kill an insect. The day his grandfather crushed a large cobalt-blue beetle under his heel, she scolded him in her Southern dialect: "*Si propriu nu stupitu. Nun capisci nente. A vita nn'ha data u Padreterno e non si può spizzare,*" which translates to "You're so stupid. You don't understand anything. God gave us life and no one can take it away." Then, when his grandfather shrugged his shoulders with disinterest, she took it up a notch, swearing with an elegant style that only a Calabrian could truly appreciate.

A family habit.

He laughed to himself, remembering his grandmother, as he entered the dining room.

The manager was speaking with some waiters. From the tense expression and nervous gestures, it was clear that he was agitated and not coping well with the day's disaster.

When he caught sight of Berté, Garaventa waved him over to a table set with a blue tablecloth, a variety of glasses, plates and sparkling cutlery plus various frills such as Easter bells and silver doves, all things that would have delighted Patty. Berté sighed as he noticed the guests in the dining room staring at his ponytail. Of course, for a five-star hotel, a detective with a certain style, a Sherlock Holmes or Hercule Poirot, would be more appropriate. Perhaps an investigator in a tailcoat and monocle, a worldly, elegant man with a gardenia in his lapel. Instead, at the Grand Hotel Miramare, they got 200 pounds of distinctly inelegant Berté, with his unruly mane and his unfashionably retro clothing,

200 and then some.

'Thanks for pointing that out, you Bastard!' thought Berté before sitting down and looking around the dining room. Was he looking at the killer, hiding in the midst of these nice families on vacation? Among the wealthy old men warming their bones in the sun of the Italian Riviera?"

"What can we get for you, Inspector?" asked Garaventa politely. "Pasta, meat, or fish?"

"Something light and quick," Berté said, dying a little inside. He was famished and the Grand Hotel Miramare was famous for its cuisine, but he didn't want to look greedy. "Broiled fish will do," he said heroically.

"Would you like some white wine?" asked the manager, sitting down.

"I would," sighed Berté with regret, "but another time. Just sparkling water for today."

Garaventa signaled to the waiter and then asked anxiously, "Any news?"

"Not yet. Let's talk about security: I have officers questioning the concierge and the staff who were present last night. I assume you have already spoken with them, but, please, explain the rules of this hotel to me. We need to determine if the killer is staying or working here or if he might be an outsider."

"At night, at the reception desk, there is a concierge and another person in charge of opening and closing accounts... Then, a porter in charge of cleaning the common areas and two others who are responsible for cleaning the kitchen."

"What time does the shift change?"

"6:00 a.m."

"Are the doors locked? Who has the keys?"

"The night concierge and the attendant at the service entrance, the door we use for goods and staff. The staff can never use the main entrance, not even after working hours and when they're out of uniform. They can only use the service entrance which, therefore, must always be accessible to them."

"Has a stranger ever managed to sneak into the hotel and spend the night?"

"No, never on my watch. Sometimes, someone claims they've lost their key or that their spouse has it and tries to get a maid to open a room for them, but no one has ever fallen for it."

"So you're saying that no stranger got in last night. Now think. It was late at night after a busy holiday. Could the doorman have stepped away for a few minutes?"

"I doubt it, our security is always professional. For us, Arbor Day, Easter or Christmas is all the same, they're all work days."

A waiter brought a pyramid of focaccia – a mix of plain focaccia and focaccia with olives and onions – that momentarily distracted

Berté.

"Is there an assistant manager?" Berté asked, reaching out his hand, unable to resist.

"Yes, but he's at home sick."

"Signor Garaventa, before the discovery of the bodies, did any of the guests step out of the hotel for any reason?"

"I asked about that. The doorman says he remembers that Signor Polledo, a guest who goes for a jog every morning, went out around eight in the morning and returned around nine. Then there was Colonel Badeschi, who always goes out early to buy a newspaper in the village. Even on a holiday like today, he doesn't break his routine. Finally, Signor Gomez went out early and came back around ten. I've written it all down, but there might have been others. That's just what the doorman remembers."

The manager handed Berté a sheet of paper.

"I can't assure you we didn't miss anyone. This morning all hell broke loose, and it's entirely possible the doorman was distracted. We don't make our guests punch in and out."

"Of course... we'll do our own checking as well. What can you tell me about Signora Van Der Meer?" he asked, wiping his greasy hands on a napkin. The pyramid of focaccia was now only a memory and a few crumbs but it had improved Berté's mood immensely and he now felt he was at the top of his game.

"I only have good things to say. An exquisite woman, a philanthropist. Many charities in the area receive donations from her. Not only that, she has also helped people in need who've been recommended by Caritas or local parish priests. She also supports cultural associations, you know, no one donates anything for culture anymore..."

Berté listened, astonished. His first impression of the perfumed countess had been very different. "Good for her!" he exclaimed. "Does she reside in the hotel permanently?"

"Yes, except for the summer months, which she spends in South Africa. She doesn't like the chaos of the Italian Riviera in August and she takes the opportunity to go and check on the mines that Count Van Der Meer left her. But I think she has personal reasons as well. The countess is quite attached to South Africa, at least from the way she talks about it."

"Does she have family there?"

"A stepdaughter. I met her when she came to visit last year. A real lady and the wife of a diplomat. I don't know about any other relatives she may have."

The waiter arrived pushing a trolley that included a large covered tray that, once uncovered, revealed a fish coated in salt. The waiter expertly removed the crust to expose the steaming sea bass inside. A delectable ocean scent wafted over the table. Berté felt his mouth begin to water. He found himself in front of a plate with the most delicate – and whitest – fillets he had ever seen, surrounded by a rainbow of baked vegetables. His meal was a thing of beauty, a work of art. The fish tasted even better than it looked. For a few moments he and the manager ate in silence.

"Outstanding! Truly outstanding!" Berté felt compelled to exclaim, once he had finally finished. He had to physically restrain himself from standing up and applauding the chef.

"I'm pleased you enjoyed it. Would you care for something else?" the manager asked eagerly, signaling to the waiter.

Ha-ha. You know you have to lie, don't you?

"No, no…" Berté lied, who would have happily devoured at least two more sea bass and an entire pan of focaccia… plus dessert. "Just a coffee, thank you. That's the one thing I can't give up."

While they waited for the coffee, Berté mentally shook himself and got back to business.

"What kind of relationship did Signora Van Der Meer have with her staff? Good? Any disagreements? Did they ever argue?"

"No, as far as I'm aware, they got on very well."

"Did the victims celebrate Easter here, or were Sommariva and Ferrari allowed to spend the holiday with their families?"

"Here. The countess doesn't like to dine alone. Signor Sommariva and Signorina Ferrari always dined with her and claimed to enjoy doing so."

"And you were in the hotel last night when it happened?"

The manager stared at him in shock. "Why are you asking me?"

"Routine question."

"I was at home with my wife and family."

"Until what time?"

"You are asking me for an alibi." the manager said, swallowing bitterly with a drawn expression.

Berté waited silently.

"We had dinner and watched a movie," Garaventa replied in one breath, "Then I went to bed. My wife will be able to testify that I also read a book for at least another half hour."

"Good, but you misunderstood me. I just wanted to know if there was someone from the management present at the hotel, that's all…"

Ooh. Aren't you the clever one.

"Let's get back to our victims," continued Berté. "I must ask about a delicate subject. I know you're the soul of discretion, but this is murder."

The manager nodded, trying – and failing – to cover his annoyance with a helpful expression. "Was the relationship between Sommariva and Ferrari public knowledge?"

"I knew nothing about it until this morning," the manager said with conviction.

"And Signora Van Der Meer and Sommariva only had a work relationship?" Berté ventured.

The manager cleared his throat but didn't answer.

"Come now. They've been living in your hotel for three years," Berté went on. "Do you want me to believe that you don't…" He stopped as the coffee, served with chocolate eggs and small pastries, arrived. Berté's eyes lit up. He couldn't resist sweets. He reached for the tray while the manager drank his coffee in a single gulp.

"Their behavior in public has always been irreproachable," Garaventa said hastily, placing his cup on the saucer, "What happened behind closed doors… I don't know and it's none of my business."

"Have you ever heard them argue?" Berté asked, momentarily switching tack as he swallowed a pastry.

"Never," said Garaventa decisively.

"Any rumors about their relationship among the staff?"

A brief hesitation.

"I don't like listening to staff gossip," Garaventa said icily.

Berté's eyes bored into Garaventa's. "I'll take that as a yes."

"I must respect the privacy of my guests."

"Two of your guests have been riddled with bullets and their privacy has been… well, shot to hell."

Berté's voice became flat, almost deadly, and the manager looked down at his hands.

"They were lovers," he admitted in a low voice, "but if you think that a woman like the countess would do such a thing out of jealousy…"

"Signor Garaventa, don't get ahead of yourself. What you and I think is unimportant. Evidence is what counts, and that's what I'm looking for. Any detail can be crucial, so please put your opinions aside and tell me what you know."

The manager swallowed and nodded.

"Now tell me about Ferrari's aunt."

"Signora Gianna was the countess's secretary for many years. However, about six months ago, she was replaced by her niece Ornella. Gianna suffers from a form of arthritis which prevented her from continuing in her position so she resigned and returned home. But I know she has remained in contact with the countess."

"Do you think Van Der Meer misses her?"

"I don't know… Signorina Ornella was also very efficient," he said with a small crack in his voice.

"What kind of woman was this Signorina Ferrari?"

Berté stared at the director thoughtfully. He realized that Garaventa was a lousy liar and unable to hide his thoughts from him. Berté would give some thought to the best way of taking advantage of this.

As if to validate Berté's insight, Garaventa blushed. "She had a… how do I put it? An explosive personality," he said finally.

"A very beautiful woman, no?"

"Very, very… sensual," Garaventa blurted out, refusing to look Berté in the eye and fidgeting with his wedding ring. Berté suspected the victim's attractiveness went beyond her looks and was not to be underestimated. The manager, at least, had certainly been under her spell.

"Did Ferrari have relations, let's say, friendships, with any other guests?"

"No, I don't think so… but I don't really know anything," Garaventa answered quickly. "Whenever Ferrari and the countess entered the dining room," continued the manager, "it turned a lot of heads, that's undeniable."

"Thanks, and for lunch too." Berté got up, followed by Garaventa. "I won't take advantage of your kindness any longer… for now. But be prepared: I'm sure I'll have to impose on you again."

"I'm completely at your service," said Garaventa, holding out his hand.

Berté shook it and left the dining room, his retreating form followed, once again, by the curious eyes of the diners and the discreet tinkling of silver cutlery and crystal glasses. That damn ponytail!

His chat with the manager had made him realize the need for a more in-depth encounter with that paragon of virtue, the countess. After asking the receptionist to announce his visit, he took the elevator up to the fifth floor where Van Der Meer's suite was located.

A maid in a blue and white uniform opened the door for him. She led him into the living room, where the unmistakable scent that had so unsettled him still lingered. There was soft music playing, perhaps a Mozart sonata, but he wouldn't have bet his life on it. Classical music wasn't his thing. The room, with its shiny parquet floor, was decorated with fine furniture including armchairs and sofas in pastel shades. Some handcrafted objects, apparently made by children, rested on a cherry bookcase. Perhaps they were gifts from people whom Signora Van Der Meer had helped, which would add credence to the manager's testimony.

The countess was sitting in a pink damask armchair, talking on her cell phone. Her stepdaughter, Berté guessed, as she said a fond goodbye and promised to call back. In one hand she clutched a small silk handkerchief which she unconsciously tormented, repeatedly twisting and pulling at it. She put the phone down on a table and looked at Berté, who was standing in front of her. There were traces of recent tears evident in her red eyes. With a wave of her hand — bejeweled and a little trembling, Berté noticed — she invited him to sit in the armchair next to hers.

A deputy assistant chief of police graciously allowed an audience by a Peer of the Realm!

Indeed, that was his immediate reaction even without that Bastard's prompting. A rush of plebeian anger began pumping through his veins, but he took hold of himself with both hands and resumed his dignified, good cop exterior.

"Signora Van Der Meer, I'm sorry to disturb you at this undoubtedly painful moment…"

"I'm upset, Inspector… is that what I should call you?"

The question was asked in a melodious voice. Berté felt an inner compulsion to believe that Van Der Meer was truly the angel of goodness painted by the manager.

There was no point in trying to explain that his title was correctly rendered as "Deputy Assistant Chief of Police" so he nodded. "I need to ask you a few questions, but it won't be a formal interrogation, just a chat with an informed witness."

With a slight nod of assent, she made it clear that, since she had no choice, she would comply.

Such graciousness!

"The police interrogate witnesses and people with knowledge of the facts pursuant to Article 351 of the Code of Criminal Procedure…" Berté found himself reciting in a professional tone, "The provisions of the second and third sentences of paragraph 1 of Article 362 apply…"

"Yes. Very good, Inspector, I understand. It won't be necessary to recite the entire code. Van Der Meer said dryly, a little annoyed.

Berté decided to leave it at that. At forty-two, he'd learned when to be a provocateur and when not. "First things first: did you hear anything unusual last night?" he asked. "Gunshots, unusual noises, voices?"

Van Der Meer raised her manicured eyebrows, reinforced with a line of dark pencil. "No… I retired earlier than usual because I had a severe migraine. I took a sleeping pill and fell asleep right away."

Berté thought that he and the countess had at least one thing in common: migraines.

A truly democratic affliction.

"How long have you known Sommariva?" Berté asked softly.

"Almost five years. He was in charge of managing my assets."

"How did you meet him?

"When my old financial advisor decided to retire, he referred me to the president of a well-known private bank, who introduced me to Sommariva."

"What were the requirements for the position?"

Van Der Meer stared at him perplexed, as if she were surprised by his ignorant curiosity. "Experience in managing assets, knowledge of several foreign languages, a willingness to travel, discretion and reliability. I handle my investments in-house and I require a professional who is always at my disposal. In exchange, I offer a substantial salary, as you and your hunting dogs will soon discover…" she gave him a reproachful look. "I cannot say I enjoy you nosing around in my business, but I'm not afraid of you: everything is legitimate and I pay my taxes on-time and down to the last penny."

Berté accepted the abuse with a smile. As annoying as she was, Van Der Meer fascinated him and he appreciated her frankness.

"That does you credit, ma'am, but I'm not the *Finanza*, the tax police. I deal with thieves and murderers."

Something flickered in her eyes. It was only there for a moment, but he couldn't mistake it.

It was fear.

But was it a perfectly natural fear that a double murderer was on the loose or was it something else? He had picked up a useful trick from a friend of his, Andreone Corvi, who interviewed famous authors for a living. Corvi would put uncooperative authors at ease by sharing a friendly but slightly unsettling fact about himself. "Did you know that I live in a hotel, just like you do, Signora?" Berté asked with a disarming smile.

Van Der Meer looked at him in amazement, and Berté sensed that his trick might not have created quite the impression he had hoped. She had an expressive face and, right now, it appeared to be saying, "Well isn't that special." But the countess was too well-bred to put the sentiment into words.

Nonetheless, after a sigh, she murmured softly: "Then you understand! I never liked taking care of a house. Since I've been widowed, I've chosen this life, and I am satisfied with it. I don't have to call the decorator or the gardener. And no one expects me to organize gala dinners…"

Ah, yes. Gala dinners. How does one cope?

Berté high-fived his conscience. For once he fully shared the sentiment. On the other hand, he did understand the attraction living in the hotel held for Van Der Meer. Given his limited free time, the advantages of living in a boarding house were considerable.

So you think she's having an affair with Garaventa? Because that's the attraction for you...

"Before coming to Lungariva, where did you live?" he asked quickly, hiding a smile.

"At the Villa d'Este in Cernobbio, on Lake Como."

Berté barely suppressed a whistle. Van Der Meer did not stint herself. The Villa d'Este was one of the most prestigious hotels in the world. He'd only been there once to attend the wedding of one of Patty's rich cousins.

Patty did have her uses.

"Why did you move to Lungariva?" he asked.

Van Der Meer stared at him, her face unreadable.

"I like change. After the lake, I felt like living near the sea, and the Grand Hotel Miramare is outstanding. The location is stunning and the food and service are superlative."

Berté remained silent for a few moments, returning her neutral gaze. He wanted to make sure she understood that this topic did not end with her careful reply.

"Are you an Italian citizen?" he asked, switching topics for the moment.

"I have dual citizenship, Italian and South African. This allows me to spend time in Cape Town. I still have a lot of business there and I lived there for many years with my husband. It's a wonderful place, but without Victor... Have you ever been there?"

Berté shook his head and continued: "Do you still have family there?"

"I have no children of my own, nor any blood relatives. I have many friends, and my husband's daughter whom I see in the summer months. She married a diplomat and is often traveling the world. A lovely woman, much like her father."

Berté made a mental note to call this lovely South African stepdaughter.

"Did Sommariva have any enemies," he continued, "perhaps someone who may have threatened or blackmailed him?"

A brief hesitation and then, "As far as I know, no, nobody," the countess said, a little too casually. "He was an honest and diligent man. In the five years he worked for me, I can't recall a single mistake. As for his private life…"

"Yes. His private life. What about it?" Berté pressed.

"… Well, I don't know much. He has… he had a daughter and a son, but I've never met them," she elegantly shrugged her slender, straight shoulders as if to say "Why would I?"

"And Signorina Ornella Ferrari?"

"She was my secretary, she took care of everything. She was the niece of my former secretary, who had to leave me for health reasons. I miss her every day." A hint of sadness crept into her voice.

"Why? Was her niece unsatisfactory?"

"Ornella was certainly not as experienced and efficient as her aunt, but she did her job well. I am devastated by her death."

"Did you know about her relationship with Sommariva?"

Van Der Meer looked away and adjusted her pearl necklace nervously. With a sigh, she said: "No, and if I had known…" she hesitated, "I would have dismissed both of them. I do not tolerate illicit affairs," she concluded suddenly.

"Illicit? They were two unattached adults…"

Van Der Meer stood up quickly and moved to the window of the terrace overlooking the sea. She contemplated the breathtaking view for a moment before turning back to him.

"You're judging my morals. I don't think that's part of your job. I assure you that I have not the faintest idea who could have done something so atrocious… Believe me: I am saddened and, in addition to the pain of having lost two employees that I have worked with closely, this creates many practical problems for me…" The countess's voice cracked for an instant and a look came into her periwinkle eyes that made her seem younger and more vulnerable.

Berté realized he would not get anything else out of her, at least not for the moment. Certainly, she wasn't going to blurt out that she was linked to Sommariva by anything more than a simple work relationship.

"Of course," he said, getting up, "And I must apologize for imposing on you at such a time. Unfortunately, I will have a few more questions later and I must warn you that we're going to have to dig into your affairs. The prosecutor plans to have us examine all the documents that Sommariva was working with in your office. We need to check that he wasn't engaged in any illicit activity."

"Illicit?" Van Der Meer raised her eyebrows and stared at him with hostility.

"I have no doubt your business activities are perfectly respectable and completely legal, Signora," Berté replied, "but we're investigating murder – a double murder – and we can't afford to overlook anything." Mightily struggling to resist the Bastard's urging to take his leave with a courtier's sweeping bow and much twiddling of the hands, Berté quickly retreated towards the door.

"Detective!" called a now-captivating voice. "Has anyone ever told you that your ponytail is most handsome?"

Berté stopped in his tracks, stunned. He was seldom surprised by anything a potential suspect might do, but having an elegant septuagenarian – whom he had just insulted – flirt with him over his ponytail was an entirely new experience. He should have said something, perhaps a witty aphorism or at least a thank you. But nothing came to him and he simply stood there. Eventually, he managed a weak smile and a nod before collecting himself and closing the door behind him.

Pathetic.

Yes, he was aware of that, thank you very much. He was not particularly suave, Patty was right about that, at least. But such was his nature, he mused as he stepped into the elevator. He sniffed experimentally, noting that Van Der Meer's perfume still clung to him. He ran into Gianasio in the atrium.

"Sir, there's been a development."

Berté waved her into the investigation room where officers were taking statements from the hotel guests and toward a free table in a corner overlooking the garden. "Something important?"

"I'd say so," confirmed Gianasio, smoothing her skirt. "I spoke to a couple of maids who work on the countess's floor. It seems that two days ago Van Der Meer had a scene with Sommariva. The maids heard the countess shout that 'if he didn't stop she would make him pay dearly.' They didn't hear what he had to stop, but the two assumed – *everyone knows*, they said – that Sommariva was Van Der Meer's lover and that she was crazy with jealousy."

Berté nodded. He had suspected as much. Before he could answer, the last person on earth he wanted to see at the moment hove into view in the shrubbery just beyond the window: Costa, the reporter. Berté leapt out of his chair and went to the French door.

"Costa! Get out!" he barked. Gianasio was right behind him. Unsure of what was going on and fearing the worst, she reached back with her right hand, ready to pull out the gun hidden under her jacket.

Alarmed, Costa backed away and disappeared among the plants.

"That's all we need right now. Sabatini, get rid of him!" Berté was now shouting and everyone in the room was staring at him.

"I'll take care of it, Sir," said Sabatini as he ran out of the room in pursuit of Costa.

"Damn Costa!" Berté shouted again, banging his fist on the table. "He weasels his way in where he's not supposed to be and writes things he shouldn't!"

He bent over to pick up his chair, still swearing under his breath. "Sorry!" he said, taking a deep breath, "That reporter gets on my nerves. As you were."

He sat back down, clearing his throat to try to hide his embarrassment. Gianasio also took her seat again. A little paler than before.

"Sorry, Gianasio... Listen, let's get back to what you were saying."

"No problem, Sir."

"Yes, it was. Just ignore me. I've got a short temper sometimes, but you'll see I'm all bark and no bite. Costa is a reporter and he has a way of really getting under my skin. But I usually forgive him. He's not a bad fellow, really, just a little too inquisitive. And, to be fair, that is his job. So, you were telling me that Van Der Meer threatened Sommariva. Dig into it. In a place like this, others will know about their relationship and somebody must have heard something. I also want a full report on Van Der Meer's business dealings. Our esteemed hotel manager is convinced she's a saint, but my nose tells me something doesn't quite add up. So go through all the documents in the office. Her wealth apparently comes from South Africa. South Africa means diamonds and diamonds often mean trouble. They're a little too portable for their own good."

Gianasio held up her hand. "Slow down, Sir, there's something else. I spoke to Consuelo, her maid. It seems that every evening after dinner – unless she was out for some reason – Van Der Meer went to Sommariva's room. The bartender confirms that he almost always gets an order to send herbal tea up to the accountant's suite at 10:00 in the evening whenever Van Der Meer is in the hotel. The official reason for visiting Sommariva's room was to go over the next day's schedule. The countess sometimes returned to her room after about half an hour. Sometimes she didn't return to her room for hours."

"So Sommariva wasn't just a bookkeeper. He was a full service accountant! But why didn't he make the trip to her room instead?"

"From what the maid said, I gather that the countess cares a lot about keeping up appearances. So naturally, she didn't want a man visiting her room. And anyway, she justified her evening visits on the grounds that any documents that needed to be reviewed were already in Sommariva's suite, which was also the accounting office."

"Interesting. That changes things. Did the maid also admit that Van Der Meer and Sommariva were lovers?"

Gianasio gave a hint of a smile. "She and several others."

"And did the herbal tea ritual take place last night too?" Berté asked.

"Indeed it did. I checked at the bar: herbal tea went up to Sommariva's room at ten o'clock. The champagne was ordered around 11:30. It seems like the 'cheating lover' motive is..." Gianasio trailed off as she caught sight of the team from the morgue and two suspicious bags.

Two to check out.

The room fell silent as the two corpses passed. Several people stood up. The tension was broken when a phone rang. Gianasio, who had chosen "Stayin' Alive" as her ring tone, began frantically rummaging through her bag.

One of the forensic technicians walked over to their table.

"Sir, we're checking the room for fingerprints now, and we'll have a report as soon as possible. We're sending the gun to the lab along with the computers and all the documents."

"Be sure and get the phone logs," recommended Gianasio, who had quickly ended her call.

"Their last messages aren't difficult to follow," continued the technician, "Sommariva texted Ferrari just before 11:00 to let her know that the countess had gone to sleep and inviting her up for a drink. Ferrari replied 'I'm there.' There are also some earlier messages. As soon as we've gone through them, we'll have the report on your desk."

"Make sure you include the time stamps on the messages between Sommariva and Ferrari. They're important," Berté ordered.

The technician nodded and walked away. Gianasio resumed her report. "OK. Now listen to this. The woman who was working at reception claims that yesterday afternoon a man in his fifties came to the hotel asking for Ferrari, but she refused to meet him. The guy then went to the bar and after about an hour she saw him leave. He looked furious – and drunk."

Berté rolled this new information around in his head. There was definitely something here. "Does the receptionist remember his name?"

"Unfortunately not. She only recalls that he was well dressed and that he had drunk a lot at the bar."

"Talk to the bartender and work on the phone records, he and Ferrari may have been in contact with each other before. Anything else?"

"No, but we still have a lot of people to question. Tell me what you meant with your 'that changes things' in regards to the countess."

"Let's reconstruct the events of last night. Sommariva and Ferrari have dinner with the countess. Then Ferrari goes to her room, and Van Der Meer and the accountant go to his suite to drink herbal tea as usual. But she has a headache, or something, and returns to her room. As soon as she leaves, Sommariva gives Ferrari the green light and she joins him for a champagne toast. Eventually, the murderer arrives – the coroner will tell us the approximate time – opens the door with the key, perhaps the master key stolen from the distracted maid, unloads the entire magazine on the two of them, probably by the light from the hallway, throws the gun under the bed and leaves, closing the door. The killer was not a professional, otherwise two shots would have been enough. Instead, and this confirms the killer's agitation, he or she fires almost wildly and riddles them with bullets. But there is another possible explanation: perhaps the killer did not want to kill Ferrari, but Van Der Meer. Perhaps the killer expected to find her in Sommariva's bed, rather than the secretary. Both are blondes, and in the semi-darkness there could have been a mistake."

Detective Gianasio nodded, and said: "It's a reasonable theory. But how did the killer know he would find them both in bed asleep? Here's another theory: the jealous Van Der Meer suspects her employees are having an affair. She pretends to have a headache and retires to her room. Then, a couple of hours later, she uses her key to sneak into Sommariva's room — I verified she has a copy. She catches the traitors in bed, terminates their employment, and goes back to her room."

"It's certainly possible. There's both motive, and the opportunity to enter the room without breaking in, but there's something about Van Der Meer's personality... I can't put my finger on it, but it makes that improbable..."

"But the killer must know the hotel and the staff's habits well if he or she was able to steal a key from the hotel office and use it to sneak into Sommariva's room."

"The killer certainly doesn't seem to have improvised, but it's too early to tell. The killer entered the room using a key. Coincidentally, that evening, a maid lost her master key and didn't notice until the next morning. I don't believe in coincidences. We need to get her to talk."

"I already did. She's terrified. She knows that her job is hanging by a thread. The manager has already given her an epic chewing out. But I'm not convinced by your theory. I think it does look like a coincidence. My theory is certainly simpler. Van Der Meer had her lover's room key. And a motive."

Berté said nothing for a moment. Detective Gianasio had already drawn her conclusions, and they pointed straight to Van Der Meer.

"I agree that the killer is living or working at the hotel," he said finally, "but I don't want to start with an assumption that could lead us astray. We must act quickly, however. This is a hotel and potential suspects are going to start disappearing soon. So we either catch the murderer immediately or this case will end up on the list of unsolved crimes. By tonight, secure all the telephone records and start reviewing them. The quicker we can collect the evidence, the better."

"Fine. I'll get back to work, then," said Gianasio with a tired smile, getting up from the table.

Parodi, who had been hovering in the background, now approached Berté. He seemed to be annoyed, cranky. That was unusual.

"What is it, Parodi?" Berté asked.

"It's just that, all these *Genovesi*... I... I..." he stammered.

"You...?"

"I can't stand those bastards!" he snapped. "They're arrogant, obnoxious, condescending..."

Berté interrupted him with a thunderous laugh, which made several heads turn.

"Parodi, let it go! We have a ton of work to do."

"You say that because you haven't had to deal with *them* yet." He gestured as if to say 'I know what's what!'

Berté suppressed a grin. Belli had told him about an incident involving Parodi and an inspector in Genoa. They had quarreled over a trivial matter of jurisdiction and Parodi had been chewed out by his superior, who had taken the side of the inspector. Parodi might be just a sergeant, but when it came to holding grudges, he *had* no superior.

"Sir, about that Garaventa..."

"You found something?"

"Not exactly, it's just a feeling... He seems so refined and polite, but when it comes to the staff... Look, I understand that keeping a place like this running properly requires ensuring that your employees have complete respect for your authority, but something's not right. I was in the kitchen when the detective from Genoa..."

"You just can't bring yourself to call Gianasio by her name, huh?"

Parodi shrugged to show his disinterest.

"When the *detective*..." Parodi resumed contemptuously, "was questioning the chef, Garaventa, who was present, had him terrified."

"Really!"

"Yes, Sir, that was my impression."

"Maybe he does have something to hide."

"Everyone seems perfectly honest and open but underneath..."

"It's always the same story," sighed Berté. "Talk to the people who left the hotel this morning before they found the bodies. I have to swing by the police station. You stay here and call me if anything comes up. I'll be back in half an hour." He turned away before Sergeant Parodi could reply. However, before he could reach the door, an elderly man stopped him, grabbing his arm tightly.

"Are you the detective in charge of the investigation?" the old man asked. His tone made it seem more like an accusation than a question.

"Yes," Berté replied dryly, extracting himself from the stranger's claw. He could not stand it when strangers put their hands on him. It was a pet peeve he had carried with him since childhood. He stepped back a couple of feet to observe the man. Tall and lean, dressed impeccably in black, he held a cane with a silver handle. His wrinkled face was capped by an incredible mass of white hair. Two slightly watery eyes stared at Berté.

"I've been saying that sooner or later something would happen!" the old man barked. "I warned Countess Van Der Meer, but she wouldn't listen! She only sees the good in people... I never liked those two, they pretended to love her, but they were only with her for the money."

"And you are...?"

"*Commendator* Olindo De Cillis," the old man exclaimed proudly.

That meant something, thought Berté. De Cillis had been awarded the Italian equivalent of a knighthood. "Do you know Signora Van Der Meer well?"

"For two years now. I, too, live here during the winter. We often chat, Licia and I... Look, Inspector, modesty aside, I've known many women in my life, I'm eighty-seven, you know, and I've been married twice, but I've never met someone like the countess. Besides her beauty, she's also generous and cultured. She traveled the world, when the world was still an acceptable place, unlike the way it is now..."

"Why do you say you suspected something was going to happen?" Berté interrupted him, fearing that he was about to go off on an extended tangent about the good old days. "Did you see or hear something?"

"I've seen things... and also heard things…"

"Such as?" Berté nudged.

"It's not just what I've seen and heard. It's also the impressions that I have gotten… That secretary! A real piece of work who was out for what she could get. No man was safe from her. And Signor Sommariva, who still considered himself a young man, was putty in her hands. She probably would have gone after me if I'd let her have a sniff of my wallet! This must have hurt Licia deeply..." the *commendatore* lowered his voice, "Licia was smitten by Sommariva, a handsome man, for all his bad judgment, and good at his job, but I was sure he was cheating on her."

Berté sighed. He was wasting his time, De Cillis didn't know anything that wasn't already in his file, but he wanted to feel important. That can happen to anyone who used to be someone, as they get older, Berté reflected. Old age robs one of the limelight, and not everyone copes with the loss. Berté was looking for a polite means of escape when a man in his fifties came running up. He was not very tall, had very light hair, fine features, and blue eyes.

"*Commendatore*, please! I've been looking everywhere for you!" he said, a reprimand in his voice.

"I was assisting the inspector with his investigation!" the old man replied with impressive dignity.

Berté nodded, giving the younger man a pointed look.

"Well... well, now it's time for your medicine."

"He's my caregiver," De Cillis said witheringly. "My children sent him to keep an eye on me and he won't leave me alone for a minute, but I can take care of myself perfectly fine without his... assistance."

The look the younger man gave Berté as they left spoke volumes. Berté made his way to the hotel lobby but stopped again. No, this was not the time to deal with the press. He made inquiries at the reception desk and then snuck out a back entrance like a thief... or a murderer.

As he left the hotel, he popped his coat collar and ducked his head to conceal his identity, took a *caruggio*, a medieval lane too narrow for cars, and made his way to the police station.

The case was difficult, perhaps the most difficult of his career, given the number of possible suspects. But also thrilling, and for the same reason. The prime suspect had to be Van Der Meer. But how could she have gotten her hands on a weapon like that? He had a hard time imagining her negotiating the purchase of an illegal weapon in a shady back alley somewhere. Of course money can get anything done, but the countess would have almost certainly needed an accomplice... She was not someone you were likely to forget, even if you just saw her once.

Berté felt his heart begin to race with the thrill of the chase.

Woot! Woot! Code Red! High blood pressure alert!

His conscience had a point, he thought. He should probably get that checked. Once upon a time he didn't give a damn, but now he wanted to be in good shape for Marzia. Dear God! He could not wait for her husband to board his ship so he could…

Stop! Stop right there!

No way! No way in hell I'll stop!

He couldn't resist. Ducking through an alley, he changed coursed and headed for the Pensione Aurora. Finally a bit of luck. Marzia was at the reception desk. Alone. They looked into each other's eyes for an instant. Berté suppressed an urge to jump over the desk. The lobby probably wasn't the place for that.

"Luigi, how nice to see you!" Marzia greeted him while remaining behind the counter. "Any news?"

"No, I only came to… to…"

"To see me?" she asked in a low voice.

Berté said nothing. Looking around to check that there was nobody in the lobby, he leaned over the counter and kissed her on the lips.

"I'll take that as a 'Yes'." Marzia said, laughing and flashing the perfect teeth that Berté had always admired.

"Marzia, I wanted to talk to you about something. I had wanted to do it properly but it looks like this case is going to be a nightmare and…"

"Don't worry about it. There's no rush."

"There is for me. Look… I'll just say it. I don't picture myself as a home wrecker and I don't want to be responsible for ruining your marriage!"

Marzia stopped him before he could continue. "Yes. I suppose I need to speak to you, too. But this isn't really the right moment, or the right place! Soon, though." This tender moment was interrupted by a loud ringing. Berté hastily removed his phone from his pocket. Shit. It was Terani, the chief of police, who, no doubt, wanted an update on the investigation, something Berté would have already done had he gone to the police station like he was supposed to.

For once, he beat the Bastard to the punch. 'I'm an idiot,' he thought, 'Here I am, flirting with a married woman when I've got 2 dead bodies and 137 suspects to sort through.'

Sheepishly waving goodbye to Marzia as he briefed Terani on what had happened that morning, he made his way out to the street and hurried off in the direction of the police station.

*****

The atmosphere at the station was not business as usual. Almost all his officers were at the Grand Hotel, consumed by the investigation. As he was the first person with any authority to sign anything they had seen all day, he was immediately assaulted by every administrator in the building, each one having questions that needed to be answered and papers that needed to be signed. He did his best for a few minutes but soon retreated to his office, closing the door behind him.

He rubbed his eyes and vigorously shook his head, causing his ponytail to flail about. He wasn't tired, exactly, but the sheer volume of work ahead of him and the need to find this killer quickly weighed on him. He picked up his phone and asked for a coffee, which, when it came, turned out to be very bad. Parodi was the only person who could ever get the espresso machine to produce anything drinkable. Proper Italian espresso has a *crema*, a delicate, light-brown foam hiding the thick, almost jet-black, coffee beneath. He examined the thin, flat, brown liquid that lay in the bottom of the plastic cup with disgust, morosely recalling the porcelain china and the excellent cuisine at the Grand Hotel Miramare.

He sighed and drank it anyway. Perhaps he was becoming one of those stereotypical detectives in mystery novels, he mused. They were usually caffeine addicts and lovers of good food, excessive drinkers but not quite alcoholics, heavy smokers, unlucky with the women in their lives, with troubled pasts, etc., etc. Well, stereotypes came from somewhere, he supposed. Surely there was at least one fictional detective that wasn't fanatical about *arancini* and whiskey, who had a quiet and happy childhood, who ate regularly, didn't smoke, and had a normal wife that he adored. A fictional detective who was a perfectly nice, uncomplicated person and yet still had the creativity and intelligence to solve crimes and the fortitude and guts to bring the bad guys to justice. When you thought about it, this was an odd tradition because the father of them all, Inspector De Vincenzi of Milan, while a complicated man, was a paragon of self control.

Funnily enough, he had actually known someone exactly like this at the real Milan police headquarters: a seemingly unremarkable man, courteous and reserved, but when he sank his teeth into a case you could be sure that he wouldn't give up and that sooner or later the culprit would be caught. And when the case was finally closed and the killer brought to justice, he went back home to his wife and played with his children.

To be perfectly honest, now that he thought about it, that *was* unusual. People who devoted their lives to pursuing murderers were seldom "normal."

I'd like to introduce Exhibit A for the prosecution, Your Honor.

He had to admit the Bastard had a point. No one would ever mistake him for completely normal. For one thing, he talked to his conscience. Even worse, he had a secret vice, writing. It was such a secret that nobody, except Marzia, knew about it.

He turned to the computer on his desk and with one hand, pushed a good-sized hill of paperwork out of the way. The urge to write the story that had flashed through his mind that morning when he should have been examining two murder victims was rapidly eroding what was left of his will power. 'Only ten minutes,' he convinced himself, 'enough to distract myself and clear my mind...' Murder suspects aren't the only people who lie to police officers. For once, the Bastard had nothing to say.

*****

His "ten minutes" had become almost an hour when his phone pinged with a text from Marzia. Shaking his head, he saved what he had been working on – he couldn't call it a story yet – picked up his phone and read,

"Love forbids you not to love
The soft hand that rejects me
Once sought the warmth of mine;
Your eyes declare your love,

And what is this?" thought Berté. It certainly wasn't one of the haikus that he and Marzia often exchanged. It seemed more like... something from an opera? Perhaps, but which opera? Not one of the few he was familiar with, certainly. And the meaning? No, after a second reading, he understood the message, but which opera it was from remained a mystery. He was about to type the lines into Google when his phone pinged again with another text from Marzia.

"And don't try to google it! Where's the fun in that?"

Berté smiled. She had read his mind once again. It was a little embarrassing to be caught like that but even more embarrassing to be predictably lazy.

What sort of person knows the entire libretto of every opera ever written by heart?

Feeling extremely guilty, Berté typed the verses into Google and immediately found the answer: *Fedora*, a three-act opera by Umberto Giordano.

He had never heard of the opera or the composer. But, since Marzia never did things without a reason, Berté decided to read a summary of the plot.

A shiver ran down his spine.

"On a frigid night in St. Petersburg, the Russian Count Vladimiro Andrejevich is shot dead by a stranger's pistol... Countess Fedora Romazoff, his betrothed, decides to find the culprit and seek her revenge."

That Marzia! She never ceased to amaze. He responded with what he thought was a very clever text that made no mention of his research.

"We'll see it together. My hand, however, won't reject you... On the contrary!"

Pleased with his wit, he dove back into the reports on his desk while ignoring the Bastard's grumbling complaints.

He was just finishing up a witness statement when the phone on his desk rang. It was Parodi. It seemed that Sommariva's daughter had arrived at the hotel and he wanted to know if he should send her along to the station. Berté instructed Parodi to hold her in the investigation room until he arrived. He got up, put on his coat and headed off for the Grand Hotel.

It was beautiful to stroll along the boardwalk, through the gardens in which, in addition to a sculpture – if it could even be called that because it was made of aluminum and canvas, and Berté had never really liked it – towered a statue of Christopher Columbus, his arms stretched out toward America.

Columbus was a distinguished Ligurian, at least as far as Italians are concerned. Berté had heard that Spain and Portugal also claimed him as one of their own. Perhaps the world's greatest explorer was good for tourism. 'The Americans stole the telephone. The Germans stole blue jeans. Now they won't even leave us Columbus!' though Berté bitterly.

During the summer, retired people lounged on the benches, breathing the sea air and contemplating the stunning view of the gulf and the boats that decorated it. Children chased each other by day in the same square where concerts and shows were held at night. There were worse places to spend his exile than Lungariva. Next to the "Church of the Boats," as Berté called it because of the numerous ship models it contained, was the fish market. As he caught the market's distinct aroma on the breeze, Berté noticed an older woman dropping what looked like a shopping bag full of clothes into the yellow Caritas donation bin and another man who was letting his dog drink from the nearby fountain. Berté smiled. Lungariva wasn't just a playground for countesses, regular people enjoyed living there, too.

And how, where, and most of all with whom, would he spend his old age?

Ha-ha. You aren't even sure where and with whom you're going to spend the next month.

Perhaps the Bastard had a point. It was hardly the moment for such questions. He quickened his pace, intent on reaching the Grand Hotel and resuming the investigation.

After a hurried word with Parodi, he introduced himself to the accountant's daughter, "I'm Deputy Assistant Chief Berté." he said, smiling politely.

The woman raised two dull eyes. She was tall and very thin, her gaunt face framed by a dark bob. Very elegant and timid, at first glance. "Pleasure, Alessia Sommariva." she responded.

Berté shook her thin, ring-adorned hand and invited her to sit across from him. Gianasio was the only one in the room and was questioning two of the hotel's maids. Berté envied the speed at which she typed on her brand-new laptop. He, instead, trusted his memory and wrote everything down after completing an interview.

"Signora Sommariva," he began, forcing his face into a sympathetic smile, "I am so sorry to meet you under these circumstances. I'm hoping we can have an informal chat about your father. Any background or information you can give me will be of great help in our investigation. Can you tell me anything you know about his last few days? Was he worried about anything, for instance?"

Alessia Sommariva nodded and crossed her legs, covered by gray leggings and tucked into black knee-high boots. "I'm afraid I don't have much to tell you. I live in Milan and I haven't seen my father in three years."

"Three years?" Berté was astonished.

"Yes. That was when my son was born. He made the effort to come and see his grandson but couldn't be bothered to come all the way to Milan again after that."

"Are you married, Signora?"

"Yes, I'm a housewife."

"And your husband, what is his occupation?"

"He has a car dealership in Milan."

Berté carefully observed the grief concealed in her eyes. She was not as indifferent as she seemed. Berté tried to estimate her age. From her face, he would have guessed she was over forty but her extreme thinness made it difficult to tell.

"Am I to understand that there was bad blood between you and your father?"

"We ignored each other. My parents separated many years ago. My brother and I were raised by our mother, who passed away ten years ago. My father was never around, and we got used to that. We saw him only on big occasions. Now that I think about it, not even many of those; he didn't bother to come to my wedding. My brother walked me to the altar."

"What do you know about the work your father did for Signora Van Der Meer?"

"I know that they met six years ago. I remember because it happened shortly after my brother Paolo... disappeared."

"Disappeared?" asked Berté, suddenly hearing a metaphorical alarm bell sounding in the distance.

"Well, I lost track of him, anyway. The last time I heard from him was about two years ago. I got a postcard from India. He had decided to cut his ties with his old life. He said he was well, that he didn't have any intention of returning, and he asked me not to look for him."

"Did you search for him?"

"No, Paolo is a weird guy, unique... he was interested in philosophy, and India always attracted him. He considered it an ideal place to pursue his studies. So I respected his decision, even though it gave me grief. We were close once."

'Strange family,' thought Berté.

"Let's get back to where we left off: six years ago, just as your brother left for India, your father..."

"My father decided to resign from the finance company he had always worked for and follow the countess."

"Follow... what do you mean?"

Signora Sommariva gave him a pitying look.

"He never admitted they were lovers, but I knew. My father was a charming man, and well aware of it. I've never met the countess. But I know that she is older than him, and that she is extremely rich, and I know my father..."

"Well, you'll get to meet her now."

"Yes, I asked the doorman for her, but one of your officers intervened, and told me that I needed to see you first."

'Well done!' thought Berté.

"Did your father have other relationships after your parents separated?"

"I don't know. Again, my father was practically a stranger to me. He wasn't involved in our lives. He didn't even pay child support. Fortunately, we could do without him. My mother inherited several properties in Piedmont."

"And she never claimed what she was owed?"

"Our mother never asked for help, and she taught me to do the same." Alessia responded proudly.

"That's because she could afford to," Berté pointed out.

'It's easy to keep your pride when you're swimming in money,' he thought. 'When you aren't, though, you have to take your pride and stuff it...'

Expressing our inner Bolshevik, are we?

The Bastard was right. What the hell was he doing, baiting a witness like that? He was letting his personal quirks interfere with an investigation.

However, Alessia Sommariva didn't seem to resent his attitude. Instead, she smiled at him, saying, "You're quite right. Fortunately I have never wanted for anything, apart from a father. And I didn't even suffer that loss all that much. But I think it was different for my brother. In fact, I think that's why Paolo left. He was furious with my father as a child and even as an adult, he never came to terms with that. He usually referred to my father as 'the asshole.' As far as I know, Paolo hasn't married. Maybe he was scared of becoming an absent parent himself. Who knows?"

Alessia Sommariva was giving him precious information about her family. The metaphorical alarm bell was now an air raid siren. Somewhere out there was an estranged son who hated the charming accountant because of his childhood abandonment... did he hate him enough to kill him?

Berté returned to his interrogation. "Did your father ever talk to you about his relationship with Signora Van Der Meer?"

"As I've already told you, no, he never talked about it. In the few phone calls we had, we usually talked about my brother... and that usually ended with me accusing him of being responsible for his disappearance. Of course, he didn't agree."

"Okay, Signora Sommariva," he concluded, "that's enough for now. Can we ask you to stay in contact with us in case we have any more questions?"

"Yes, your colleague's already discussed that with me. I have a room here in the hotel."

They shook hands, and Berté once again noticed her sad gaze. Wealthy, yes, but abandoned by her father, now without her mother, with a brother who had fled to India...

Every unhappy family is unhappy in its own way.

He watched her leave. She was a striking woman, but, in his eyes, nothing exciting. Too skinny. Too cold.

Your tastes have changed.

Undeniably true.

'The mechanisms of attraction are strange,' he thought, but he didn't have the time to further explore this theme because he saw Parodi approaching, accompanied by a woman. For a moment, Berté's heart stopped.

Patty?!?

No, it wasn't her, but he had never seen such a resemblance! Same hair, same eye color, style of dress, the same designer bag... even the same slightly unnatural gait, like a runway model. Was it possible that she really looked that much like Patty? Or was his guilt over their breakup playing tricks with his imagination? Was he going to start seeing her around every corner now?

You're diagnosable, is what you are.

He shook his ponytail and braced himself. He smiled at Patty's doppelganger and extended his hand saying, "Deputy Assistant Chief Berté."

In response, the blond burst into sobs and fell into the chair.

'Dear God. She even acts like Patty! The same hysterical reactions...' thought Berté.

"I can't believe it, I can't believe it..." she murmured between sobs, holding her head in her hands and rattling her bracelets on her left wrist. "My poor sister..."

Berté looked at Parodi in mute appeal. He didn't really want to take responsibility for trying to console the Patty look-alike himself. Parodi came to his rescue, handing her a tissue and asking her if she wanted a glass of water.

It took a few minutes for the victim's sister to calm down. Finally she pulled herself together and was capable of coherent speech. "Claudia Ferrari," she said with a last sob.

Berté mentally pushed play again on Bereaved Relative Tape #1. "I am so sorry to meet you under these circumstances. I'm hoping we can have an informal chat about your sister. Any background or information you can give me will be of great help in our investigation. Can you tell me anything you know about her last few days? Was she worried about anything, for instance?"

"I hadn't seen her for a while. I live in Turin, and she was here in

Lungariva ever since she took over Aunt Gianna's old job, my father's sister..." she stopped to blow her nose.

Berté watched her quietly, trying to dispel Patty's ghost.

"The countess trusted our aunt," continued the woman, "and our aunt was very fond of her. She stayed with her as long as she could, not just because she was fond of the countess, to be honest, but because she enjoyed the travel and living in luxury hotels. But six months ago she began having some health troubles so she decided she'd had enough. Fortunately, she's saved up a bit of money over the years so she's now comfortably retired."

"I see. Could you please provide contact information for your aunt to Sergeant Parodi? We'll be following up with her as well. Can you tell me a little bit more? Did she get along with the rest of the staff?"

"Aunt Gianna is very pleasant and flexible, as you have to be if you work for the countess."

"What do you mean? Is Signora Van Der Meer difficult to work for?" asked Berté.

"No, that's not what I meant, exactly. The countess, for what little I know, is always kind, and everyone holds her in high regard, but it's different when you work for her, that's what Ornella said. You must go where she goes and live where she lives. That's not always easy. But you also give up any thought of a private life or a family. There's no Christmas or Easter with your family. You get very few days off. She never wants to be alone and your presence is required. She doesn't accept substitutions, not even at meals. So every lunch and dinner, you must always smile and entertain her. You follow her to the theater, to conferences... You're not just a secretary, you're her shadow. Your work day never ends and you always have to smile and say 'Yes, ma'am!' no matter what she requests."

"Did your sister tell you this?"

"Yes, of course."

She started to cry again. Fortunately for Berté, Claudia Ferrari didn't sound very much like Patty at all. Otherwise, the interview would have been unbearable.

After the crisis had passed, Berté continued. "So, when your aunt went into retirement, Signora Van Der Meer hired your sister to replace her."

"Yes, she wanted someone she could trust. Ornella..." Her voice broke and ground to a halt.

"Please continue, Signora…"

"I was saying that Ornella wasn't married, she graduated with a degree in Foreign Languages, something that Signora Van Der Meer required… She was about to lose her job anyway because of cutbacks so she was the ideal candidate."

There was something there. Berté could smell it. "So why was Claudia chosen as the new secretary and not you?"

Claudia Ferrari blushed violently. Apparently this was, indeed, a sore subject. The two sisters had been rivals for the job which, despite Ferrari's description, was still a golden opportunity, especially for a young woman at the beginning of her career.

"Me? No… I would never have accepted the position." she responded quickly, "I would never have walked away from my business. I have a very successful boutique in Turin and going to university would have been a waste of time. I have lots of friends. And I certainly would never have left my boyfriend, not when he's finally on the verge of asking his wife for a divorce! No, I have a wonderful life. Ornella, on the other hand, was under a lot of pressure. It wasn't just losing her job, it was that she didn't want to get married and she was having a bit of a meltdown. She wanted to get away for a while, a change of scenery."

"She was having a meltdown because she didn't want to get married? Why? Marriage isn't a necessity anymore." asserted Berté.

Are we talking about you or Ornella Ferrari?

It seemed to Berté that Parodi was now giving him a sympathetic look, but he decided he was imagining it.

"You don't understand," continued Claudia, sparing him from further embarrassment, "Ornella was in a serious relationship, but she wanted out of it and joining the countess gave her the perfect escape."

"The name of this man?"

"Antonio Brioschi."

"They lived together?"

"No! My sister and I lived together. She wasn't in love with Antonio. She started dating him casually but he became more and more jealous, possessive. At the end, it was really suffocating. He didn't even want her to work anymore… It was hell for her! So when

Aunt Gianna proposed that she take this job, Ornella didn't hesitate. Great salary, life in big hotels, and freedom from Antonio."

"He took it well, I imagine…" Berté poked.

"Ha! He was furious when she left him. But making a clean break from him was the only thing to do. Antonio is a bit rough and not very well educated. Oh, he's successful enough. He's made good money with a couple of gyms that he owns… But he's long on muscles and short on brains." Ferrari concluded maliciously.

'Hunky Antonio must've really been something,' Berté chuckled to himself, 'but not really a *gentleman*.'

"I ran into him in Turin, about a month ago. He asked me how Ornella was, I told him that she was doing great, and he feigned indifference. He, on the other hand, didn't seem to be doing well… if you ask me, he's started drinking."

"Where does this Brioschi live?"

"In a loft somewhere in the Lingotto neighborhood in Turin."

Berté glanced at Parodi, who was furiously taking old-school notes in an actual notebook.

Brioschi could have been the man who had come to look for Signora Ferrari. A friendly chat with our Italian Stallion was going to be necessary, he mused.

"Apart from him, was there anyone else who had it in for your sister? Please think carefully. Even the smallest detail might be important."

Claudia put her head in her hands for a few moments, concentrating. "Not that I can think of. Sure, she liked to have fun… she liked… well, I'll say it, she liked her men. But she never led them on, I swear. You should talk to some of her friends, I'll give you their names, if you like. She had been talking to Laura a lot lately – I know because she came into my shop two days ago to buy a dress and she mentioned it, but…"

"Yes, please, give us the names of her friends and their contact information. That's important." Berté looked at Parodi, who nodded. "Did she ever mention her relationship with Signor Sommariva?"

"A little. She thought he was an interesting man, older and more worldly. Ornella was attracted to Sommariva, I think, but she knew that the countess seemed to have a thing for him. In fact, two or three days ago she was telling me about how the countess chewed him out for flirting with the maids. Ornella thought it was hilarious, but I knew she was very careful not to do anything to put her job in jeopardy. She even deleted text messages she got from him just to be safe.”

‘Another piece of the puzzle,’ thought Berté. By now he had a general idea of who Sommariva was. A man who liked women and who had managed to make the elderly philanthropist fall in love with him by making her feel young again. A man who also liked to live dangerously. Not content with seducing his boss, he also went after her beautiful secretary. That would have provoked the countess’s jealousy… who had procured a gun and terminated her unfaithful employees. There were still a few details to work out but that certainly seemed like the simplest solution to the case.

Perhaps too simple. It was always the details that got you.

“Well, thank you Signora Ferrari, you have been very helpful, but I will probably need to speak with you again at some point.”

“I’ll stay as long as necessary.” Tears ran down her Patty-esque cheeks, evoking a strong emotion in Berté.

“Now I’ll leave you with Sergeant Parodi. Please give him the names of your sister’s friends, as we discussed. We’ll see each other again soon. I’m so sorry for your loss.”

He couldn’t come up with anything more original to say to the poor woman, but that was nothing new. When he got emotional he could never find the right words. He sighed and took out his phone. It was time to update the prosecutor on the investigation.

He could never sit still while he was on the phone and so he began pacing up and down the room where Gianasio and the other officers were working. Gianasio seemed to be quite efficient. Unlike Parodi, he didn’t mind having her on his team at all. In fact, the moment he had finished his call, she intercepted him.

“Berté, we have an update on Sommariva’s phone.”

“And?”

“We’ve also been following up on the next-of-kin information that Sergeant Parodi collected. Sommariva has a son and a daughter. The daughter lives in Milan but the son goes back and forth between India and Italy.”

“Really? His sister doesn’t know that. She assumes he’s gone into permanent hiding in India."

"Not at all. We checked the passport records. He comes back, stays for a few months, and then leaves again. In fact, he talked to his father several times over the last few days."

"Certainly not to say 'Happy Easter'," remarked Berté.

"Probably not. There are five phone calls total, two from the father, and three from the son. About fifteen to twenty minutes each."

"Anything else from the phone logs?"

"Just some suggestive texts from Sommariva to Ferrari: he pursued her, and she played along. The night they were killed seems to be the first time they were able to "consummate" their relationship. They had been waiting for the right moment when they were free from Van Der Meer's all-seeing eye."

Berté snorted. "The right moment? They could hardly have picked a worse one."

"Yeah. I prefer a nice clean murder. I wish this one didn't involve quite so much intimate detail." said Gianasio, crestfallen.

"I don't like it either," he admitted, "but it's our job. We can't overlook any details, although I do agree with you, it's uncomfortable being so involved in the victims' personal lives."

Gianasio nodded, resolute. "Well, even if it makes me uncomfortable sometimes, I would never give up on this job."

"Because you want to make sure the bastards pay." Unintentionally, Berté's expression had hardened.

"Yeah, that's it exactly." she agreed, blushing slightly. "I've also got some news about Ferrari's cell phone. A certain Antonio Brioschi was sending her threatening messages. He may be the man who was looking for her on Easter. We tried calling his number, but he's not answering. We're checking to see if he's been at any of the hotels in Lungariva and the surrounding area. I had his photo sent over," she said, showing him a picture on her phone. A man with long, black hair, dark circles under the eyes, and strong features. A unique face, certainly not particularly refined, but rather macho.

"Send that to me," Berté ordered. "I'll see you here around dinner. Grossi will be meeting us. Let's carry on tonight until we've got a good handle on all the witness statements. People may be trying to leave tomorrow."

"I'll stay here as long as it takes. I still have ten people on my interview list and then I want to go over a few of the statements with you."

"Fine. See you later." he said, walking away. He avoided any further conversation because he had been working on his own theory and he didn't want to share it with anyone. Every now and then, he needed some time alone to work through his thoughts. All those people around, all that chaos and confusion... Parodi was right, in the end having all those people from Genoa here was a pain in the ass. In Lungariva he had gotten used to being ignored by the powers-that-be and running his little team of three detectives: Parodi, Belli, and now young Sabatini, who was quickly improving at his job thanks to Berté's merciless criticism and frequent tirades. He slipped out of the Grand Hotel quietly. Though it was already dark, many people still lingered.

The lone wolf stalks the streets seeking whom he may devour.

If you'd asked him last Easter to bet whether he'd spend this Easter in Lungariva, he would have given a hundred-to-one odds against. If you had told him he'd be spending Easter Monday walking its streets, it would have been a thousand-to-one.

He walked everywhere in Lungariva, through its narrow, medieval alleys, called *caruggi* in the local dialect, through the squares, along the boardwalk, even out along the breakwater that protected the 16th century castle from the fury of the sea.

In Milan, he had never walked a single step, if he could help it.

Milan...

Just saying the name made him feel nostalgic. He'd thoroughly enjoyed his life there... well, perhaps not "thoroughly," especially not his last few months which had been a living nightmare. It wasn't the city's fault, it was the fault of the SOBs that lived and worked there.

This fit of nostalgia made him realize he had never called back Stefano, his friend and colleague in Milan. The call had come in earlier but he'd been talking to Grossi and couldn't answer it. He dialed the number and was met with that raucous laugh that always cheered him up.

"Well, well, it's my lucky day!"

"Did you hear about this mess I have on my hands?" Berté asked.

"I heard, I heard. You can't catch a break, can you? Aldo Stabili is having a stroke, you wouldn't believe how much he envies you."

"He's welcome to it. I don't envy myself. What are you up to?"

"Ha! I'm at home. Betty and I are playing with the toy our daughter got in her chocolate Easter egg."

"How lovely!"

"What do you know about it, you old bachelor? Look… I know Patty's mad at you. She calls my wife two or three times a day to vent. What on earth did you do to her?"

"We're over, but she doesn't want to admit it."

"So you're with someone else. Don't try to deny it, I know you. And yet, you never tell me anything."

"Yeah. There's someone else, but it's not that simple," he admitted, finally saying the quiet part out loud.

Stefano remained silent for a moment, hearing the sadness behind Berté's words. "Come on now, it can't be as bad as all that, at least not yet! When are you coming back to Milan?"

"I was just there, two months ago!"

"I mean when are you coming back, as in *for good*?"

Stefano's question stunned him. For good… Suddenly feeling slightly nauseous, he quickly changed the subject and made his goodbyes as soon as politeness allowed. He put his phone back in his coat pocket and stared into the dark sea, stricken by the feeling of not really belonging anywhere. Eventually, his growling stomach distracted him from his melancholy and he started down the street, towards the center of town.

Spain… who knows why Spain and its traditional *tapas* popped into his head. You have a drink in a bar, then you nibble on something, then you head to the next bar, another drink, another nibble – and you keep going until either your legs or your liver demand that you stop.

That's just what he was going to do. An aperitif at the Caffè del Porto, a canapé from Frontini, and – why not! – a small sandwich at the Bar Milano. He could even pretend he was working. Everywhere he stopped, he would show Antonio Brioschi's photo and ask if anyone had seen him. Perhaps the unfortunate Signorina Ferrari hadn't wanted to be seen with him at the Grand Hotel and had agreed to meet him elsewhere just to hear him beg.

Continuing his tour, he stopped at the Lungariva bookstore. The shop was open, even though it was Easter Monday. Necchi, the owner, profited from tourists whenever he could, because he knew he would be in for a lean couple of months until the summer crowd descended.

Seeing Necchi in his bookstore finally dislodged the splinter that had been irritating Berté since lunchtime. The title he couldn't remember was *Death in a Bookstore*, featuring Inspector De Vincenzi.

Thank God we sorted that out. You might never have slept again.

Berté could see Necchi was busy with a line of customers so he decided not to enter. Instead, he waved him through the shop window and paused to look at the bestsellers on display. Most of the books seemed subpar – that was his modest opinion as a lover of the classics – but he was happy to see, displayed prominently, a collection of short stories written by famous authors and edited by his friend Andreone Corvi. Bookshops always made him think of his father. When his work allowed, Inspector Tonino Berté was something of a literary connoisseur. He read a lot of thrillers and detective stories but only by great authors. When something didn't measure up to his standards, he would get bored and cast the book aside. It had been his father who had suggested reading a novel about a murder in a hotel: *The Cellars of the Majestic*, by the great Simenon. In the novel, Inspector Maigret was investigating a murder that took place in a grand hotel in Paris. Berté remembered the atmosphere of the story, and the general plot, but for the life of him he could not seem to remember how the detective had managed to catch the murderer. He would've happily reread it. Perhaps Necchi had a copy? But at that moment Berté didn't want to go in and explain, so he continued on to a bakery in front of the Basilica. He often stopped there because he liked their coffee blend and they had all kinds of pastries and cakes. Feeling like Inspector Maigret in a Parisian bistro, he strolled up to the counter and asked for his usual short espresso, a *ristretto*. Perhaps it was a bit late in the day to drink caffeine, but he was sick of soft drinks, and considering the fact that he would need to stay awake for at least a few more hours, coffee was what he needed. While he waited, he showed the photo of Brioschi to the barista.

"Hmm... let me get a closer look at that..." he said, wiping his hands on a towel and peering at the photo. "Yes, that's definitely him!"

"You've seen him?" Berté asked, suddenly completely awake even before having his coffee.

"Yeah. I've seen him. And I can tell you precisely when. It was the day before yesterday, I remember it well. This guy was big, I thought maybe he was a bodyguard or something. He came in by himself and sat there, at that little table. It was almost noon and he ordered a Campari, then another, and another… to the point where I almost told him he'd had enough. But a blonde woman – quite good looking – came in and sat at his table. She ordered a drink herself, I don't remember what. After a while, they started arguing… then she left, just left him sitting there. He paid and then left as well. He might have gone after her, I think."

"You're sure it was him?"

"Yeah, positive. He has a very particular face and was the size of a refrigerator. I'm not likely to forget. People like that don't get into heated arguments with beautiful women every day, at least not in my bar."

Berté showed him a photo of Ferrari. The barista nodded, passing Berté his espresso. "Uh huh. That's her. That's the blonde I was talking about."

"Did you hear what they were arguing about?"

"No. I was working and didn't pay that much attention."

Berté paid his bill and left, walking briskly back towards the Grand Hotel. He found Parodi, Gianasio, and Grossi, the prosecutor, waiting for him, sitting at a dining table set for them in the "Torture Chamber," – as Parodi had nicknamed the interview room to much general amusement. Garaventa was already standing by to take their orders.

Despite having just returned from his "tapas" run, Berté was looking forward to a full five-course Grand Hotel Miramare dinner after his stellar experience at lunch. Unfortunately, under pressure from Grossi, they decided to keep it "light" and have a traditional *apericena*, a large tray full of a variety of finger foods. Fortunately – at least for Berté – "light" is a very relative term. Berté tucked into yet another pyramid of excellent focaccia as well as olives, chips, nuts, and slices of pizza. Their waiter refilled the tray twice before he gave up and brought an outstanding warm seafood appetizer that hinted at the culinary wonders that would have been Berté's if only the prosecutor's stomach hadn't been acting up. To Berté's surprise, Gianasio kept up with him, chatting happily and eating at the same time. A woman with a healthy appetite always put him in a good mood. Patty's non-stop dieting and her inability to really enjoy a good meal had been depressing Berté for years.

As the waiter cleared away the final plates, Grossi got down to the business of the evening. "So where do we stand with the investigation?" he said, looking at Berté. But it was Gianasio who answered. Gianasio believed that the killer was staying at or working in the hotel, since he or she knew the ins and outs of the hotel's daily routine and since all entrances were closely monitored and a stranger would have been noticed. She went on to list all the employees present on the night of the murder: the maid who had the master key stolen, the new bellhop, the night receptionist, the bartender who had brought champagne up to Sommariva's room. She even included the manager himself, who had gone home just before nine, but whose alibi was only based on the testimony of his wife. To Berté's private amusement, she made much of Parodi's observations regarding the manager and his belief that the manager was hiding something.

But at the top of her list was the name Van Der Meer. So far, the documents and files found in her office had not revealed anything suspicious. Her assets seemed to be very well managed and she seemed to be personally generous, with large sums being donated to various charities. As yet, there was nothing to suggest illegal or abnormal activity. If there was anything that might attract suspicion, it was the dizzying salaries she had paid Ferrari and Sommariva. But that did not deter Gianasio whose theory was that the murder had nothing to do with money and everything to do with sex, specifically, the love triangle involving Van Der Meer, Sommariva and Ferrari. Van Der Meer, an older woman, had paid too much money to Sommariva and had mistaken his devotion to his paycheck for love. And when the new secretary, the beautiful and available Ornella Ferrari, entered the picture, it was a combustible situation that was bound to blow up eventually. Van Der Meer, who was both wealthy and had certainly been extremely beautiful in her younger days, was used to getting her way and not the sort of person who would accept being cast aside.

Hell hath no fury.

'It makes sense, a lot of sense… and yet… and yet, something is still missing.' thought Berté. Because Van Der Meer was frightened. And he needed to figure out what – or who – she was frightened of.

When Grossi turned to him to ask him his impressions of the hotel employees, the relatives of the victims, and the countess, Berté evaded the question and focused instead on what he had learned of Ferrari's ex-boyfriend and the fight that they had on Saturday at the bar. As he detailed his evening's investigations, Gianasio's face became more and more inscrutable. Berté had a bad feeling about this. Grossi noticed it, too.

"You never learn, do you Berté?" he said, shaking his head. "Anyway, keep up the good work, all of you. I suggest you look over the last few interviews that Gianasio *and her team*" – Grossi gave a pointed look at Berté – "have so diligently compiled and then get some sleep so tomorrow you can be sharp. Goodnight!"

Berté, feeling like a jackass for not sharing his information with Gianasio before she spent five minutes detailing the bellhop's movements to Grossi, gave her an ingratiating smile. It was not returned.

The Second Day

Showers. There was nothing like a morning shower.

He would have liked to stay there forever, eyes closed, letting the stress of the last few hours rinse away as the water cascaded over his head and down his back. He was getting too old for long nights with little sleep, let alone no sleep. He had eventually made it back to the Pensione Aurora well after midnight and it was even later than that when he finally got to bed. And then he lay there, awake, waiting for sleep to come. It never did.

He shut off the water and put on his robe. The *Aurora* was certainly not the Grand Hotel, but it did have its compensations. The cleanliness was impeccable, the food incredible, and the personal service second to none.

Personal service?

He wondered if Captain Pestarino had already left… Didn't he have a ship to catch?

If Pestarino had not left the building, he resolved to act completely casual and say nothing to Marzia, despite his impatience. It simply wouldn't have been correct to have a conversation like that when her husband was liable to interrupt them at any moment. Besides, he was too much of a coward.

'I wonder if she'll be serving breakfast?' he mused, pulling on his jeans, annoyed that they were becoming increasingly difficult to button. He then chose a white polo shirt and a gray jacket from the closet. It seemed a bit casual for a police officer in charge of an important case that was drawing press to Lungariva as if it were hosting the World Cup, but he rebelled against dressing up today, a reaction that, he guessed, was due to the lavish surroundings of the Grand Hotel and its wealthy, sophisticated clientele. Dear God, those people annoyed him!

Well, they certainly annoy you now.

As you get older, your tastes change. He was getting older, certainly, and his tastes had definitely changed. Not all that long ago, he had been attracted to the skinny model type, the more unattainable the better. But he had grown to appreciate the Rubenesque charms of a woman like Marzia, not to mention her style and class. Van Der Meer had class as well, although of a different type. Elegance seemed to run through her veins, even though she was not an aristocrat by birth. And those eyes, well… their aquamarine gaze hid the secrets of an extraordinary life. Once again, he tried to imagine her opening the door to Sommariva's room and finding his two victims *in flagrante*.

Van Der Meer would have been the perfect protagonist for one of his short stories: "The Countess of the Grand Hotel" would make an excellent title. In the latest issue of the *Polizia Moderna* magazine that he had on his bedside table, he had read the review for a collection of *noir* stories set in Milan, published by a small press. The magazine also accepted stories by emerging authors. Why not submit one of his?

Ah, no. He didn't want to run the risk of rejection. Better to just wait.

Coward.

Smiling wryly, he slipped his Beretta into its holster. Though he was no longer in Milan, he hadn't gotten out of the habit of carrying it, and, seeing how Lungariva was becoming the Cabot Cove of Italy, perhaps it was a good idea after all.

A bit dramatic, don't you think?

He ignored the Bastard's sniping and picked up his coat. Outside, the sun was shining, but there was bound to be a crisp breeze. He pocketed his phone and his keys before heading to the dining room for breakfast.

He felt really good this morning. Strangely enough, his migraine hadn't bothered him for days. Only a fellow sufferer could truly understand his joy at that. How lovely to be pain free, no one hammering at his temples (depending on the day either the right or left side, but sometimes both) and not suffering from a never-ending wave of nausea. He marveled that even his sleepless night and the immense stress of trying to solve a front-page double murder against the clock had not caused his migraine to return with a vengeance. He smiled grimly to himself. Perhaps it was all the coffee he had drunk the day before… As if on cue, the aroma of fresh coffee enveloped him as he entered the dining room, an aroma blended with the unmistakable scent of Marzia.

So she *was* serving at breakfast that day. Perhaps she would smile at him…

He sat at his usual table and nodded at his fellow diners who stared back at him with undisguised interest. Either something had gone very badly wrong when he dressed himself that morning or the news had spread that he was the detective investigating the double homicide at the Grand Hotel. A copy of *Il Secolo XIX*, the biggest newspaper in Liguria, was lying on the table next to a simple glass jar that held three twigs dotted with small, yellow flowers. Berté admired them critically. They smelled of honey and sun.

Looking around at the other tables he noticed that they all had Easter-themed floral arrangements – Marzia was a stickler for the finer points of hospitality – featuring primroses and sprigs of olive.

Why then, on his table, were there these yellow flowers instead? Marzia did nothing randomly, so there was certainly a reason.

While he waited for his breakfast, he glanced at the newspaper's headlines. As he had anticipated, a double homicide in such a refined setting had shocked the country. Costa and his fellow journalists had outdone themselves, apparently interviewing anyone even remotely connected with the Grand Hotel, including the pool boy. There was a four-page center spread devoted entirely to the case. He began leafing through the pages, distractedly scanning the photos.

Son of a bitch!

Son of a bitch!

At least six columns on the third page were filled with a photo immortalizing him and Detective Gianasio at a table in the Grand Hotel Miramare. He was smiling at her, and she gazed back at him fondly. This was bad. Really bad. It was so bad that even Berté was sure they were having an affair. Steeling himself for the worst, he read the caption under the photo and sure enough, "The Grand Hotel Miramare affair is absorbing all of Deputy Assistant Chief of Police Berté's attention."

He swore under his breath. He would make Costa pay for this.

Someone has a guilty conscience.

Not at all. He wasn't concerned about his own reputation. But he was worried that Marzia would get the wrong idea.

He closed the newspaper angrily, folded it sloppily, and stuffed it into his coat pocket. He knew he would have to read the whole damn story to see what other little surprises it might contain. He took a bite of Marzia's coffee cake, then he had a few slices of buttered bread glazed with the divine bitter orange marmalade made with Marzia's own hands, those same hands that...

Whoa, there, cowboy!

No, his conscience was right, he shouldn't think about her, he should concentrate on the case.

Marzia's arrival, however, made a mockery of his good intentions.

"You must have had a busy day, yesterday," she said as she sat down across from him. She looked exquisite and she placed a hand on his arm, looking at him fondly.

"I had quite a day, too. Marco left about an hour ago for Genoa, where he'll catch a plane to London and board his new ship there. He should be gone for three or four months this time."

What a shame!

Berté hid his delight behind an idiotic smile. He examined Marzia critically and tried to detect any hint of sadness in her voice.

Is she putting on an act?

Damn his jealousy! Compulsively, he felt the pocket of his coat. Perhaps Marzia had already seen that newspaper story...

"Marzia..." he said, taking her hand and feeling his face heat up.

"Yes?"

"If you should happen to see any, uhh, photos... that is, the Chief of Police sent some extra officers from Genoa and I'm... One of my new colleagues is named Mariella." he finished incoherently.

Oh, wow.

"Is she that pretty blonde one?" she asked blandly.

Shit. She's seen the picture.

"Err, yes," admitted Berté, "but look, her husband is married!" Berté gibbered.

Another cappuccino to wash down that foot?

Dear God, why was he babbling about marriage? Wasn't Marzia married too?

"I mean, I meant... What I mean to say is..." This was not going well. "I'm not interested in her, you know, like that. We're just colleagues and she isn't interested in me..." Berté internally face palmed himself. Perhaps he should just run out of the room and try to pick up the pieces later…

"Ha! If I got jealous of all the women you meet who might want to chase after you, I wouldn't have the energy to do anything else. There's no need to worry. I can trust you, can't I?"

"You can indeed, Marzia… we, well… you and I, sooner or later… I'm… imagine if I would ever …" he fell silent, probably the wisest decision he'd made since he'd gotten up that morning. He hoped this chronic inability to finish a coherent sentence would disappear by the time he had gotten back to the Grand Hotel and begun work.

"We understand each other, don't we, Luigi?" Marzia's voice was a whisper. "You just focus on finding the murderer. You're our hero. Lungariva adores you."

Before he could answer, one of the servers, gesturing, caught her attention and Marzia stood up. But Berté grabbed her hand.

"Wait! What about these flowers?" he asked.

"Oh, yes. They're winter calycanthus. It wasn't easy to find them, you know? Have you smelled their fragrance?" Marzia bent over the flowers, completely distracting Berté and filling him with a sudden, potentially embarrassing, lust.

"Why? Why are they on my table?"

"Because they remind me of you. These little flowers are resistant to pests. They're simple and sincere, and yet they have a very… sensual fragrance."

Berté nodded without replying.

Marzia blew him a discreet kiss and went off to see what crisis the still-gesturing server was dealing with.

As Berté drank the last sip of his cappuccino, his phone pinged. It was a text from Belli. Time to get back to work, he thought as he got up and strode out of the room.

Why did he and Marzia never manage to finish a conversation? Someone always interfered, something always happened. And, of course, there had always been Pestarino lurking in the background.

I thought that you were resistant to Pestarino…

Great. Now the Bastard was regaling him with bad puns. This had "long day" written all over it.

Belli was waiting for him in the car just outside the door. Berté got in quickly and Belli drove off. Their destination was Varese Ligure and the house of Van Der Meer's ex-secretary, the apparently bedridden aunt of the deceased who was unable to travel to Lungariva because of her illness, or so she claimed.

Berté and Belli didn't talk much along the way. He mulled over the information he had collected, trying to organize his thoughts and take mental notes between responding to texts and calls. The last stretch was one curve after another, but Belli handled the narrow, twisting road like a pro.

"You've never been here, Sir?" she asked, as they entered the town and began looking for a parking spot.

"I confess I have not, but I've heard something about it."

He didn't go into details, to avoid having to confess it had been Marzia who told him. She, a failed soprano and passionate music lover, came here every summer to attend Varese's annual festival of open-air opera concerts.

"It's a rather peculiar old village," said Belli, maneuvering the car to fit into the parking spot. "Of course, you should see it from above to really understand the layout: The houses are arranged to form an ellipse. Signora Ferrari lives right in the center."

They got out of the car and, after passing an ancient tower marking the entrance to the village, they found themselves in a large courtyard.

"During the summer, they hold operas here. It's famous now, but once upon a time it was a very local affair. The people in the village used to do the entire performance themselves."

Berté nodded, pretending to be fascinated and that he didn't already know. Finally arriving at an amber-colored house, they rang the bell.

A young girl cautiously opened the door. She looked skeptically at Berté but relaxed when she caught sight of Belli with her impeccable uniform, and reassuring smile.

"Police," said Belli, belaboring the obvious.

"Please, please, come in," murmured the maid. "Signora Ferrari is expecting you."

She led them into a room crammed with antique furniture and paintings. A petite woman in her seventies, with gray hair but a youthful face, was reclining on a sofa. Her legs were covered with a plaid blanket and she was attempting to dry her eyes as they entered.

"Good morning, Signora Ferrari, I'm Deputy Assistant Chief Berté," he said, flashing his badge, "and this is Officer Belli."

"Please, make yourselves comfortable," said the woman faintly, waving her hand at two armchairs across from her. "I apologize that I can't get up, my arthritis is very bad today, and... Oh! What a terrible tragedy! What scandal! My poor Ornella!" she sobbed.

The young maid rushed to comfort her. "She's been like this since yesterday morning, when she found out," she said.

Let me cue that tape up for you.

Berté cursed internally and, this time, said simply, "My condolences, ma'am. I'm really sorry, but I do have to ask you some questions."

"Yes, yes, I understand... And the poor countess! Finding them like that... she called me, she's devastated. I've known her for twenty years, and she seems calm and unruffled, but inside she suffers. She's sensitive. She has done so many good things for everyone, myself included, and she hired my niece as a favor, too... and look what happened! Ornella in bed with Sommariva! I still can't believe it."

"Did you know they were lovers?"

"Not at all! Who could have guessed? I knew that my niece had a boyfriend, but she had left him when she started working for the countess. I had told her, if you decide to work with the countess, forget your personal life. But Ornella had told me she wanted out of the relationship and was looking for a reason to break it off with him ... I think his name was Tino... Anyway, she was looking for a change."

"Have you ever seen him?"

"Tino? No, never."

"But you knew Sommariva. What did you think of him?"

"I have... I had the highest opinion of him. A courteous man, good at his job, we got along very well in the two years we worked together. I can't say a bad thing about him except this... this..."

"Do you recall anything about your niece's life that could be useful? Anything at all unusual?"

Ferrari remained silent for a moment. "No, Inspector," she said, shaking her head, "nothing comes to mind. Ornella was a good girl, this I can promise you. I don't understand how this happened... I am only thankful that my poor brother and his wife are dead and don't have to endure this…" her voice broke.

"Did Signora Van Der Meer ever comment on your niece?"

"Only to compliment Ornella. Before I retired, I had coached her for two months. She was a smart girl and she learned quickly."

"Signora Ferrari, were you aware of the relationship between Sommariva and Signora Van Der Meer?

The woman quit wiping her eyes and simply stared back at Berté.

"It's no secret," Berté encouraged her, "I only ask for any little details you might be able to add. I already know the answer."

"It was my job to respect her privacy and I never intruded on that privacy in all the years I worked for her. But under the circumstances…yes," she admitted in a low voice, "they had an intimate relationship, but it was very discreet."

"How discreet?"

"I've never seen them in public or in private acting in a way that would make you suspect a relationship other than between employee and employer."

"Interesting. Were you aware that, a few days ago, the countess was involved in something of a scene with Sommariva? Apparently she was upset that he paid too much attention to the hotel maids. Did your niece ever mention that?"

"No, she didn't say anything. But it might not have been jealousy. The countess is wonderful, but she doesn't tolerate duplicity or vulgarity. For example, she simply cannot abide crass comments about women, even if they are "compliments." Perhaps she disapproved of something she had overheard and she lashed out…"

"Is she temperamental?"

"No, that's not the right word to describe her. But she certainly isn't a person who lets things slide. I'll say it again, offensive people, especially people who are offensive or disrespectful towards women, are a pet peeve of hers."

Berté nodded. "Did your niece have any enemies?"

"No, I don't think so and I couldn't imagine why she would."

"Did Signora Van Der Meer?"

"I doubt it. She's too generous and kind to have enemies. Everyone always loved her."

"How did you become her secretary?"

"Ahh! Well, twenty years ago, I took a trip to South Africa to visit some friends. They introduced me to the countess and we immediately hit it off. She was looking for a trustworthy person to become her assistant, someone who spoke English and who didn't have any family obligations. I never married and, at the time, I was working in Turin as an employee in the HR office of a large company. It wasn't particularly fulfilling and I hated the winters so when the countess proposed that I stay in South Africa and work for her, I decided to drastically change my life. When the count died and she decided to leave South Africa and travel the world, I went with her. I've never regretted that. The countess wasn't just my employer, she is my friend."

"And in the last twenty years, Signora Van Der Meer never settled down anywhere?"

"I suppose it depends on what you mean. The countess has her house in South Africa, but she only stays there in July and August. Before she began staying at the Grand Hotel Miramare, she liked 'being a vagabond,' that's what she called it, and she would travel a lot. She loves big hotels… she says they make her feel safer."

"What does she do when she goes back to South Africa?"

"Well, she has business interests there. She inherited some mines from her husband. She also has family there, her stepdaughter, Christine. She's a really sweet woman who's always considered the countess to be her mother… She has two children, so the countess has grandchildren there as well, and she dotes on them."

As he listened, Berté examined the room, which contained some nice furniture, a few decent paintings and some photographs. One in particular caught his eye. Despite his effort to be inconspicuous, Ferrari noticed his interest.

"It's a memory I hold dear," she said, gesturing at it. "The woman in the middle is Christine. It was taken in South Africa during one of our annual visits."

It wasn't so much the sight of the three smiling women, one beside the other, that attracted Berté's attention, but rather the fact that Van Der Meer and her stepdaughter were each holding a rifle.

"Is Signora Van Der Meer a hunter?" he asked, nonchalantly.

"No, she didn't hunt. The count was an accomplished competitive marksman. He was on the national team and almost went to the

Olympics. It became a family hobby.”

“So she’s a good shot.”

“Oh yes. Both she and Christine have won competitions. She’s got quite a few trophies in her house in Cape Town.”

Suddenly, the penny dropped and the ex-secretary stopped abruptly, a look of horror on her face. “You aren’t thinking that...? No! It’s absurd, Inspector. How could you imagine such a thing!”

“What’s to imagine? She had a motive and you’ve just confirmed that she knows how to handle a gun.”

“No, no! I’m telling you that it’s impossible! I don’t know who killed Ornella, but it definitely wasn’t the countess!” Her voice became shrill. “She loves me! She couldn’t have done this to me! Ornella was my niece!” She turned to the maid, who stood at a respectful distance. “Miriam, bring me the blue folder in my desk drawer. I’ll show you, Inspector, what a wonderful woman the countess is.”

As soon as the maid put the folder in her hands, Van Der Meer’s ex-secretary opened it and pulled out several sheets of parchment paper.

“Look, Inspector, look at how many commendations and letters of appreciation she’s received,” she exclaimed, passing him a handful of documents. “Look at all these charities. Take a look at this picture. The countess never liked being photographed, but the children of the orphanage wanted something to remember her by and she agreed to pose with them. Read for yourself what they wrote to her. Oh! Ornella, and now the countess, too! It’s too much.”

She burst out in a heart-wrenching cry that made Berté feel as if he were torturing her. While the Ferrari sobbed into her handkerchief, Berté read through what she had handed him. As far as he could tell, Van Der Meer was a dedicated philanthropist who had donated quite a lot of money to dozens of charities. There were lots of letters of appreciation, but only a few pictures. One of them slipped out and fell at Signora Gianna’s feet. It was a black-and-white photo of two girls on a ship.

“Oh! I had wondered where that had gotten to,” she exclaimed as Belli picked it up and passed it to Berté. “Look how young the countess was... This was taken on her first trip abroad.”

“What do you know about her life before she met Count Van Der

Meer?"

She spent a moment staring off into the distance as if trying to remember. "I know she was born in the Friuli region and that she was orphaned during the war," she finally said. "As far as I know, she has no living relatives in Italy. She was raised and educated by nuns. Once she became an adult, she went off to seek her fortune, just as so many young girls did in the years after the war. For her, that meant going to Argentina where she still had a few distant relatives. I believe she got married to a cattle baron or something. They had no children and when he died, she was still quite young. She was well-off at that point so she began traveling. She settled down only after she met Count Victor ... It was true love."

"How did Count Van Der Meer die?" asked Berté.

"Cancer, poor man... he suffered in the end, and she was his devoted nurse. Please believe me. The countess is a genuinely good person."

"And when the count died, the countess started traveling again," Berté pressed on, trying hard to ignore the pleading look in her eyes.

"She did. She's an energetic and intelligent woman. Everything intrigues her. You cannot imagine how many places she visited! She could have been a travel writer." she confirmed, wiping her tears with her handkerchief.

The moment the handkerchief covered Signora Ferrari's eyes, Berté struck, slipping the picture into his pocket instead of back into the folder. It wasn't really a rational decision, more of a compulsion. He supposed he could have simply asked to keep it but he didn't want to offer explanations that he didn't have. Even as he did it, Berté realized he would have to give it back at some point and that was going to be embarrassing. But it was done now. He'd come up with some way to justify his actions later.

Or you could just keep it. What's a little theft compared to murder, ehh?

Berté got up, followed by Belli. "Thank you for speaking to us, Signora Ferrari. Here's my card. Please let us know if you think of anything else that could be useful." he said as he shook her hand warmly.

"I'd like to be at the funeral. I don't know if I'll be able to walk, in my condition, but I want to be there for my poor niece. I'm sorry, I didn't offer you anything... Would you like a coffee?" she asked with a voice full of sadness.

Berté would have gladly accepted, but he couldn't afford the time. He politely declined and made his goodbyes. He would also have gladly toured the village. Van Der Meer was not the only one who found new places intriguing.

A curious tourist? That's a new one.

He had noticed a medieval arched bridge that seemed interesting, but with the pressures of this case, it was not the moment. As they walked back to the car, however, Berté could not resist stopping in front of a doorway from which wafted an incredible aroma. Painted above was the legend, L'osteria du Chicchinettu. He peered into the dining room topped with stone arches. It was nothing fancy, but very atmospheric. His nose (and his stomach) were telling him that this place deserved further investigation. He promised himself to bring Marzia there, perhaps after attending an opera.

Belli caught the dreamy look in his eye and laughed. "Your instincts are as excellent as ever. L'osteria du Chicchinettu has been around over a hundred years and it's famous for its local specialties. Well, maybe famous isn't the word. It's actually something of a secret. It doesn't advertise and caters to locals. But foodies visit here from all over Europe."

"I know what you're thinking, Francesca," Berté said, getting into the car, "and if it weren't 11 o'clock and I didn't have a case to unravel, I'd certainly invite you to lunch."

"I'll take a rain check," Belli said, starting the engine and driving off. "I have a feeling that we'll be back here soon enough."

"You saw me, didn't you?" said Berté, glancing at Belli.

"Yes, of course I did... But I assume you had a good reason." she responded as Berté removed the photo from his pocket and began examining it.

The drive continued in silence. Berté appreciated her discretion. In any case, if she had asked for an explanation, he wouldn't have been able to give one. He found he enjoyed the frisson of being on the wrong side of the law, though it certainly wasn't the first time he had bent the rules. He carefully studied the two young women in the photo. The background included the sea, cleft by the wake of a large ship moving at speed, and a large lifebuoy inscribed with the word "Augustus." Both in their twenties, they were smiling as the sea breeze rippled their floral cotton dresses. They could have been sisters, both blonde and light-eyed. Van Der Meer was very beautiful, tall and lean, and the other girl slightly curvier. They seemed happy to be launching themselves into an unknown future, perhaps because their pasts and the world they were leaving behind had known such misery. What was it about this image that intrigued him so?

He sighed and slipped it back into his pocket. Best to forget about it for the moment. He distracted himself by discussing the case with Belli and explaining how the afternoon's investigation should proceed.

As soon as he set foot in the police station he could hear shouting coming from his office. As he reached for the handle, the door burst open and he was thrust aside by the menagerie of people and animals that came flooding out. First out of the door was a rather extravagantly-dressed man with long hair, a fuchsia coat, and a yellow silk scarf. Next up was a distinguished looking, yet flustered, gentleman who was immediately followed by an extremely large German shepherd. An agitated Sabatini brought up the rear.

Three men and a dog ... perfect title for a short story.

Berté was flabbergasted. "What's going on here?" he asked. Everyone began talking at once.

"Sir, they stormed in and I couldn't stop them!" babbled Sabatini.

"Inspector, this man stole my dog!" shouted the extravagantly-dressed man.

"Inspector, this man is a lunatic. He ought to be locked up!" said the distinguished gentleman.

"Arf!" said the dog, probably just to get his share of attention.

At least one of them is making sense.

Berté lost it. "Enough!" he shouted, abandoning any pretense of professionalism. "All of you clowns get back in my office. NOW!"

Momentarily stunned by Berté's outburst, they fell silent and followed him back into the office, including the dog, who, somewhat less disconcerted, was now wagging its tail.

Sometimes being an asshole pays. I've always said so.

Now firmly ensconced behind his desk, he let his temper off the leash. "Are you out of your mind? This is a police station! And you..." he glared at Sabatini. "What use are you if you're not doing your job? Who… Who… Who let the…"

Stop. Please don't say it. I beg you.

Stuttering to a halt, Berté smirked, in spite of himself, which made him appear even more deranged to the assembled crowd.

"You see, Inspector," began the extravagant man, "this… gentleman stole my dog, but he refuses to admit it!" he pouted childishly, his face assuming an absurdly comical expression.

"That's not true! I've had this dog for the last six months!" claimed the distinguished gentleman, whose complexion was now an unhealthy shade of puce.

"But he used to be mine! I lost him three days before going to Saint-Tropez for my gallery opening, but the moment he saw me again, he jumped on me and licked my face, isn't that right, Fluffy?"

A German shepherd named Fluffy?

"It's not Fluffy, it's Diablo!"

Oh, dear. From bad to worse.

"Don't listen to him! Fluffy would never forget me! He's mine! Give him back!" shouted the extravagant man.

This was unbelievable. With all the problems he had and with the prosecutor on the way, he had to spend his afternoon as some sort of canine King Solomon? He took a deep breath.

"Don't you have some sort of certificate or a license, proving your ownership? Does the dog have a microchip or a tattoo or something?"

"I repeat. He is mine, Inspector!" The extravagant man began shrieking like an operetta tenor, "he has a mark on his right eyebrow, look for yourself. You'll see!"

"Nonsense! There's nothing wrong with his eyebrows!" shouted the distinguished gentleman, who was becoming less distinguished by the minute. Sabatini, anxious to get the situation under control, began examining the dog's head. "There's nothing there," he reported.

"Ah ha! See?" the now undistinguished gentleman exclaimed triumphantly.

"But he recognized me, I'm telling you!" the other claimant shouted.

Berté's head began throbbing, as if it were about to explode. He raised an accusatory finger and opened his mouth to speak but no words came. Fluffy/Diablo had leaped onto his desk and begun licking him in the face.

Aww. Somebody has a new friend.

Sabatini jumped forward to pull the dog back. Having been now rejected by Berté, Fluffy/Diablo turned his affections on Sabatini.

"OUT!" Berté shouted in his best parade ground voice, jumping to his feet and cursing fiercely. "This is a police station, not a kennel!" He began mopping his face with a handkerchief.

Of course, that was the cue for Grossi, the prosecutor, to enter, stage right. Sabatini barely managed to restrain Fluffy/Diablo from visiting his affections on the stunned Grossi and began dragging out the now rapturously excited dog. As the two claimants left the office, Berté shouted, "Work it out yourselves. One of you needs to get another dog!" and slammed the door behind them. "I'm so sorry, Dr. Grossi!" he said, inviting the prosecutor to sit down. "You know how unreasonable dog lovers can be!"

The prosecutor didn't comment and remained stony-faced, giving Berté the suspicion that he, too, was a dog lover.

Nice one!

The meeting lasted for 45 minutes. The prosecutor, after hearing the results of Berté's latest inquiries, reiterated that he believed the countess was the prime suspect and that she should be formally questioned. For Berté's investigation, this would have been a disaster since Van Der Meer would then lawyer up and be legally entitled to refuse to cooperate with him. Now Grossi was speculating about formally arresting her…

It's true there was plenty of circumstantial evidence that she was the killer. She had the motive. She had the room key. According to Berté's new information, she was perfectly capable of obtaining and using a gun. But, as yet, there was nothing directly linking her to the crime. And Berté was far from convinced in his own mind that Van Der Meer was actually guilty.

But this was not Berté's first rodeo and he had learned long ago that it was never a good idea to argue directly with prosecutors. So with a raised eyebrow here, and a question there, Berté set about persuading him that the case was more complicated than he had originally thought. Eventually, Grossi grudgingly convinced himself that there was still insufficient evidence to formally question Van

Der Meer and that Berté's investigation could proceed. Berté walked Grossi out of the building and once they had said goodbye, he headed off towards the Grand Hotel.

A little sea air and a little exercise would do him good. He never had a case in a luxury hotel where they served coffee with fine pastries and where everything was so refined and civilized. A double murder at the Miramare seemed surreal, like a grotesque piece of post-modern performance art.

Ha! You're getting soft in your old age!

He took a detour down to the harbor and watched the boats rocking on the wind-rippled sea. The sun was pleasantly warm. Although it was only the end of March, here in Lungariva the sun was strong and healthy, at least when it bothered to peak out from behind the clouds, and not at all like the pale, sickly sun in Milan.

So much for civic pride, you traitor.

Indeed. He sighed heavily and took out his phone to call Marzia.

"Well, this is a surprise!" she exclaimed.

"I wanted to hear your voice."

"How are you?"

"Surprisingly well. Despite the dog, I didn't even get a headache."

"Uhm, right… I'm happy for you!" Marzia enthused, apparently used to Berté's non sequiturs.

"I guess Lungariva's air is good for me."

"So you don't miss Milan?"

"No, not really. But I've had better days. I'm in deep water with the investigation, and when I can get away for a moment, you're never alone…"

"I know, but knowing you're here is enough for me."

Berté remembered the tantrums Patty threw when they couldn't see each other. They were draining, but he had to admit they were also flattering. Marzia never threw tantrums.

"We have to talk," he asserted.

"Yes, we will." said Marzia, cutting him off. "Did you eat yet?"

"No, not yet. I'll just grab something… and please don't tell me what you made today!"

Marzia's laughter made him feel good. "As it happens, I'm glad you called, Luigi. I wanted to tell you something about your case."

"Tell me."

"I have a subscription to *Storia in Rete*, the history magazine. In the new issue there's an article about an infamous case, the Trigona murder. Have you heard of it?"

"No," Berté admitted reluctantly. It always unsettled him, just how well informed Marzia was. "What's the connection?"

"I don't know. Maybe nothing. But listen: One day in March 1911, two lovers rented a room at the Hotel Rebecchino in Rome. He was a penniless aristocrat and she was a married noblewoman, lady-in-waiting to Queen Elena. If you can imagine, she was Tomasi di Lampedusa's aunt, the author of *The Leopard.* Anyway, the two had been in love for months, causing a scandal both in Palermo, their hometown, and at court. But that day, the scandal got even worse. After stabbing her… well, to give you the gory details, after cutting her throat, he shot himself in the head. He didn't die, however, and was convicted of murder. He served out his sentence and even lived on for a few years after his release."

"Lovers, murder-suicide, and hotels are a classic combination." Berté commented.

"While reading the article, I thought about the Miramare case… Is it possible that it's a similar situation?"

"I can't go into the details, but it would have been a neat trick. The conditions at the scene preclude suicide, though you're half right, there was certainly a murder. But it's an excellent thought. Are you trying to steal my job?"

"No, no," answered Marzia laughing "it's not for me. In fact, I don't know how you manage to deal with such horrible stories every day."

"It's a job, but it's not easy. That's why I eat so much… to forget!"

Marzia laughed again. "There are worse vices, right?"

"Let me read that article anyway, it sounds interesting."

"I'll keep it for you. Now I have to go."

Berté thought he heard her blow him a kiss, but perhaps it was just his imagination. He pocketed his phone and resumed his return to the scene of the crime, the Grand Hotel Miramare.

He needed to put his life back in order after the disaster in Milan. He also needed to clarify his relationship with Marzia and to break up once and for all with Patty. Why couldn't he find the courage? Patty was in love with him, true, and she was beautiful and cheerful.

But she was also an overly-possessive pain in the ass. He had moved to Lungariva for a fresh start, but perhaps there was more of his mother in him than he knew. Every so often, she would have this sudden urge to clean. And when she did, she turned the house upside down. All the drawers and closets got emptied and she filled bags with things she had decided were no longer wanted and were to be given to the church. But soon enough, the frenzy passed and she would return to her old, easy-going self. The bags of stuff she was so desperate to get rid of then sat around for weeks, even months. Some of them never did get discarded. During the holidays he often thought of her.

He consciously pulled his thoughts back to the case but the image of the two cold bodies in the bed, two bodies that had been all too alive just a few hours earlier, made him shudder. Death always made him shudder. He remembered an old song by Herbert Pagani, "Albergo a ore" – "Rooms by the Hour." He started humming it to himself: *They left in perfect silence, leaving only the two bodies in the bed.* It was a poignant song, sung by the bartender of a squalid hotel renting rooms by the hour in which two young lovers had chosen to commit suicide together. A hotel room was the ideal place for unhappy lovers who chose to end their life, he thought, but it hadn't been like that for Sommariva and Ferrari.

Someone had decided for them.

When he entered, the reception of the Grand Hotel was buzzing. In the lobby milled a crowd of people who had come to satisfy their morbid curiosity. Behind the counter the staff took a constant stream of calls from potential guests, horrified by what had happened, who were cancelling their reservations. It took all kinds, Berté supposed. Parodi joined him in the 'Torture Chamber' where they had been conducting interviews and together they sat down at a table. The sergeant had a report on some of the people he had questioned.

"You know, Sir, when I think that a murderer is hiding among the people in this hotel…" he began, "it sounds just like an Agatha Christie novel."

Berté couldn't hold back a smile. Did Parodi also read mysteries?

"If he's still here, you've got to admire his guts," the sergeant went on, "but it must be extremely stressful for him. One false move, like checking out early…"

"So, Monsieur Poirot?" Berté asked, who genuinely respected his colleague but could not, nonetheless, resist the opportunity to tease him.

"So I checked through the reservations."

An excellent idea, thought Berté, who motioned him to continue.

"Here is the list of those who are checking out tomorrow: there are no sudden departures. No one has checked out early, at least not so far."

"Maybe our killer does have guts. He knew we would come to investigate and he may have foreseen that we'd consider that suspicious. We'll have to go back to the beginning." Berté began thinking out loud. "Was the crime premeditated? Or did he happen to find himself in the ideal situation to kill? If he used the master key stolen from the maid to enter the room, it probably wasn't premeditated. It's not easy to steal a master key and there would be no way to be sure that the maid wouldn't notice it was gone until it was too late. Hours passed between the theft of the key and the murder… But the killer did have a weapon. He or she must have brought it with them. The killer certainly didn't find *that* laying around in the staff break room.

"So what if the loss of the master key has nothing to do with the murder? Perhaps the killer had access to a key already and wasn't relying on a lucky accident." Parodi hypothesized.

"Could be. That still leaves several suspects. The countess had a key, but the manager and the doorman have one as well. Not to mention the cleaning staff."

"Exactly," Parodi agreed. "On the other hand, if the killer is a hotel guest, he can't wait to get out of here quietly, without attracting attention…"

"Unless the killer is still here and planning to take out someone else," mused Berté. Parodi stared at him wide-eyed. "If it was a hotel guest," Berté continued, "all we would need to do is run a gun residue test on the suspects' clothes. Our killer may well not know that you can run a test to see if someone has fired a gun recently and may still have the clothes he or she was wearing at the time of the murder. However, I don't suppose we can confiscate the wardrobes of all hotel guests, so we must have some real evidence that points to likely suspects before we can run our test. If, on the other hand, the killer is aware of this test, it's likely he or she would have taken a shower and then looked for a way to get rid of the incriminating clothes. Since you can't make a fire in the hotel without triggering an alarm, and nobody dumped any clothes in a hotel trash bin, our killer would have needed to go out with a bundle to throw it away... But where? We'll have to sift through all the dumpsters around the hotel and check if the people who went out early in the morning were carrying anything with them."

"I doubt that the murderer threw the clothes into the sea. There are always people at the port, and that would have attracted attention. People would probably have thought it was littering. There would have been a scene."

"Who knows, Parodi? But it's true. If our killer did manage to discard the evidence in the sea, we aren't going to find it. So let's give the dumpsters a try. Remind me, who left the hotel that morning?"

Parodi sighed, not looking forward to the afternoon's work. He took out his notebook and began to report. "As you suggested, we followed up with everyone who left the hotel that morning for any reason. The first on the list is Pablo Polledo, an Argentine. Handsome guy, very fit. Blond, blue eyes, so good looking he could be a movie star."

"Is he the one that goes jogging?"

"Yeah, that's him. He had a small backpack when he went out early yesterday morning. The guy has been here for a few days with his fiancée. He's been invited to a birthday party in a villa belonging to one of his clients in Portofino, a guy he trains horses for. He seems to be a phenomenal polo player. He hangs out with the rich and famous, all the fancy people who can afford to play that sport. Strange people…"

"Strange, Parodi? When you don't like something, you say it's strange. They play polo, like others play tennis, or soccer, so what's the problem?"

Parodi made his usual grimace which meant 'I disagree, but whatever you say,' and then went on. "Polledo says he didn't know Ferrari and Sommariva. I verified that by cross-checking the other interviews. Apparently, they've never even spoken with each other. In the morning Polledo goes jogging, then he hangs out with his girlfriend. She's a model," said Parodi, checking his notes. "They go out, go shopping, visit friends in Portofino and in the evening they visit restaurants and clubs." Parodi's voice held a clear note of disapproval.

"He's young, he's got money and looks, he knows the right people... do you want him to say the rosary all day?" needled Berté.

Parodi shrugged and continued, "On Easter Sunday, Polledo and his girlfriend were invited for lunch to a friend's house, David Ingraffia, who does PR for the dance club on the seafront. That evening they returned around nine. His girlfriend says that they spent the whole evening in the room together watching a movie and then fell asleep. I have no evidence either confirming or contradicting this."

"And the other guests?"

"There is another South American. His name is Luis Fernando Gomez. Sixty-four years old but in great shape, strong physique, graying hair and dark eyes. He speaks Italian because he imports Italian products for his supermarket chain in Uruguay. He says that he was invited by a fellow countryman who is opening a restaurant in Rapallo. His friend advised him to stay in Lungariva, and he gave him the right advice, if I may add my own opinion, Sir."

"Did you check if it's true?"

"Everything seems to check out. Gomez left at 8:40 to go to Mass in the small church by the fish market. The doorman doesn't remember if he had any bags when he left. Then, in the afternoon, Gomez went to his friend's place in Rapallo. I noted the time: the doorman called him a taxi at 3:30 p.m. Gomez returned at 7 p.m., before dinner."

"Anything else?"

"He is not a man who goes unnoticed, of course... He is booked for another two weeks, I checked, and he also showed me his return flight ticket."

"Anyone else?"

"Colonel Badeschi. Seventy-five years old, straight as an arrow, always at attention. He is a widower. He used to come here for the holidays with his wife, but he still has friends and memories to come back to. He seems to be sweet on Van Der Meer. And the same goes for De Cillis. He describes her as he would the Virgin Mary. They play bridge together when the countess isn't busy. He also went out early yesterday, as he does every morning, to go for a walk and buy the newspapers. We don't know if he had something in his hands when he went out. When he came back to the hotel, he found... us and the whole mess. He knows how to shoot, Sir, he gave me a lesson in ballistics. I couldn't stand it anymore, and besides, he treated me like a new recruit. But he is anything but senile, indeed, quite sharp, I would say, even if boring."

"And how long is he staying at the Grand Hotel?"

"He must have money because he, too, will be staying another month, before going back to his home in Cremona."

"Next?"

"Commendator De Cillis, the one who has a caregiver because he shows signs of dementia, but he left the hotel after our arrival."

"I met him, too. He says he had warned Van Der Meer about her staff's disloyalty."

"He went on the same tirade with me, but while he was speaking his caregiver kept shaking his head to let me know he was rambling."

"You never know, sometimes they ramble, but other times they notice details that we missed."

"I also phoned Ferrari's girlfriends in Turin. They had no useful information because they hadn't heard from her for a long time. Everyone's impression of her is that she was happy with her new job and that she was sick and tired of her fitness freak of a boyfriend."

"Okay, Parodi, don't leave the hotel. While I'm waiting for Gianasio, could you please ask someone to bring us coffee and some of those pastries?"

Parodi smiled and walked away.

He knows who he is dealing with.

Sipping his coffee, Berté googled for images of the Grand Hotel Villa d'Este in Cernobbio on Lake Como. He had stayed there, though certainly not paying out of his pocket. He had been invited to the wedding of Patty's wealthy cousin. Patty was very excited at the idea of a society wedding and had tormented him for months about the suit and tie he was supposed to wear. Villa D'Este was a charming place, in the middle of a lake that could have been painted by Leonardo da Vinci... But lakes always reminded Berté of rheumatic pains and places to cure nervous exhaustion.... He did not know why. He made a quick calculation. The wedding had been four years ago, so in all likelihood, Van Der Meer was still living at the Villa d'Este at the time. What a coincidence! They might have met each other back then, without knowing that in the future... Berté dialed the number of the hotel.

"This is Deputy Assistant Chief of Police Berté, from Lungariva. Can I please speak to the manager?" he asked the receptionist. After a few moments another voice was on the line.

"Good morning, Sir, I'm the manager. I read the papers so I guess the reason for your call. Poor countess, she must be distraught."

"You know her, then?"

"I know her very well. She stayed with us for two years and let me tell you, she is a great lady.

"So you also knew Signor Sommariva?"

"Yes, a very polite man... I was shocked when I read about his death."

"Can you tell me anything notable or unusual about their stay? For example, did they pay their bill regularly?"

"Yes they did. And nothing unusual comes to mind."

"Nothing out of the ordinary ever happened during their stay? Arguments between them, arguments with the staff... Any threats?"

"Absolutely nothing. The countess is a particularly discreet person, believe me."

After thanking her, Berté ended the call, mentally reserving the option of sending someone up to Lake Como if necessary. And now he had to make another, more difficult, phone call. His English wasn't very good, and Count Van Der Meer's daughter, Christine, if he remembered correctly, probably didn't speak Italian. He would ask Gianasio how her English was, maybe he could palm the call off on her…No sooner had he completed the thought than he heard the sound of Gianasio's unmistakable accent in the hallway.

"We looked good in the photo in *Il Secolo XIX*, don't you think?" she asked him mischievously as she entered the room and sat down in front of him.

Berté spread his arms in resignation, trying to minimize the incident. "Costa is always following me, but usually he doesn't take pictures. This time he really crossed the line." he said.

"My husband called me immediately. You have quite a

reputation…" Gianasio winked.

Berté inartfully changed the subject. "So, did you find out anything?"

"Yes, I have a few things to report. First of all, the janitor responsible for the common areas of the hotel has only been working here for a week. He is a relative of one of the women who work in the kitchen. They're both originally from Ecuador. The manager, Garaventa, told me that he hired him in a hurry because he had found himself short-handed. We checked him out. His residence permit is in order, no criminal record… He seems to be clean."

"Did he also have a master key?"

"No. He only cleans the corridors and the common areas. He needs to be available at night, but he doesn't enter the guest rooms. But it's true that it's easier for one of the staff to access the office and steal a key."

"Does he have any connections of any kind with Ferrari or Sommariva?"

"So far I haven't found anything."

"What else?" Berté asked.

"I was able to speak confidentially with the headwaiter, who is a great gossip and knows a lot about the staff. Among the many interesting things he told me, it turns out that a bartender, named Silvio Frilli, is a habitual gambler and often asks his colleagues for money to cover his losses. He only returns the money he borrows months later and only after repeated solicitations on the part of his creditors. It won't surprise you that nobody is willing to lend him money anymore. Garaventa doesn't know but only because the other employees don't want to get him fired. They feel sorry for his family. In the last month, however, he has not asked anyone for money. It appears that several people have seen him talking to Sommariva. According to our friend the headwaiter, the rumor is that Frilli asked him for a loan. Again, this is rumor and speculation."

"Did the headwaiter seem reliable to you?"

"Well… Let's say that he has a chip on his shoulder when it comes to Frilli, but in my opinion, he's not just making this up. I've gotten parts of the same story from other people as well."

"Have you talked to Frilli?" asked Berté.

"Of course. He didn't enjoy it much, he's a nervous type, you probably noticed that as well. He's the guy with the dark hair and mustache. He gives the impression he's hiding something. And he was on duty the night of the murder. He's the one who brought the herbal tea up to the room and then later, the champagne. When we spoke, he kept his eyes down and gave very short answers. I've already instructed someone to look into his movements. Frilli says that he often talked to Sommariva, but only because they got along with each other well. He claims that he doesn't owe anyone money and he's never asked anyone for money. He claims the other workers hate him and spread these rumors to ruin him."

"It is possible Frilli may have turned to Sommariva for money." speculated Berté. "It seems unlikely to me that he would have tried to borrow money from Ferrari, but we can't rule that out. We're pretty sure he knew about the affair so it could be blackmail. But that does seem to conflict with the apparently friendly relations between Frilli and Sommariva. Anyway, let's keep an eye on him. Given how nervous he is, he may step in it and reveal something interesting."

Gianasio nodded and continued, "Among other things, he was the last to see Sommariva alive – apart from the murderer, of course. He says the countess had asked the usual herbal tea, while the accountant had ordered a cognac. The countess was sitting in an armchair and she seemed to have a headache. She had her hands on her temples. Sommariva seemed perfectly normal, he even gave him a decent tip. The countess didn't say anything, apart from thanking him."

"Did he meet anyone in the hallway while bringing up the drinks?"

"Not that he recalls. He claims that every night is the same in the hotel. But he does remember that after an hour or so, Sommariva called the bar again and asked to bring a bottle of Krug champagne. He went up to the room again with the champagne, but this time Sommariva didn't let him in. He took the bottle at the door so Frilli couldn't see who else was in the room. He thought perhaps the countess was still with him.

"Hmm. Crosscheck the timetables thoroughly." ordered Berté. "And keep after him. Perhaps he'll remember some other interesting little details."

"And now the *pièce de résistance*: Van Der Meer reappeared in the dining room for breakfast today. She hadn't left her room since yesterday morning."

"Okay. But that's not really…"

"Wait for it! Our countess called the manager and asked him to contact an agency because she wanted to hire a bodyguard."

Berté could not hide his surprise. That woman was afraid, even terrified, he thought. He had sensed it during their first encounter. But why? What were they overlooking? A sensation of inadequacy took hold of him.

"So now there's a bodyguard standing in the hallway in front of her room." concluded Gianasio.

"Yeah. That is an important detail. I'll go to see her myself. Listen, Gianasio, how's your English?" asked Berté casually, baiting the trap.

"Pretty good. Why?"

"I was going to call Signora Van Der Meer's stepdaughter, but now I've got to go talk to Van Der Meer herself. So maybe you should do it. Don't let her know her stepmother is our prime suspect – or that she was having an affair with one of the victims – but press her for as much information as you can. I believe her name is Christine…"

Gianasio now saw the danger, but too late. "Fine. I'll do it." she sighed.

"Thanks, and be sure to give me a full report." ordered Berté, trying – and failing – not to smirk. Berté nodded at Detective Sergeant Gianasio and headed to the reception to inform Van Der Meer that he was going up to see her. He asked Parodi to accompany him.

The bodyguard was a young man dressed in black and leaning against the wall next to Van Der Meer's door, arms folded. When Berté and Parodi left the elevator, he stepped in front of them, but not so much threatening as inquiring. He had apparently been informed of their visit.

"Are you the deputy assistant chief?" he asked Berté, scrutinizing them both. "Can I see some ID, please?"

Parodi looked at him incredulously, but Berté simply flashed his badge and motioned for Parodi to do the same.

"Thank you," said the young man, stepping aside. "The countess is waiting for you."

Wordlessly, Berté stood in front of the door as the bodyguard knocked and the maid opened it. It was nothing personal. The guard had behaved impeccably. But Berté didn't like security guards of any description. He had no idea why.

They entered the room to find Van Der Meer on her feet, dressed in dark blue and very elegant but with a drawn face. Her light blonde hair, thick and luminous, was collected atop her head, not a strand out of place. The scent of her perfume filled the air. Van Der Meer raised her hand and, for a moment, Berté feared she would expect him to kiss it. Hand-kissing was definitely not his thing but a friendly handshake seemed, somehow, vulgar under the circumstances. Fortunately, she merely pointed to the small armchair to indicate where he should sit. Berté breathed an internal sigh of relief as Parodi took a chair on his left.

"Would you care for a drink, Inspector?" asked Van Der Meer, clearly including Parodi in the offer.

"No, thanks," Berté answered for both of them. "I see that you have hired a security guard," he continued without preamble. "Why is it that you don't feel safe, even with all of my officers in the hotel?"

The countess raised her chin and gazed directly into his eyes. Her blue – very blue – eyes were almost glowing. But the look she gave Berté wasn't icy. Far from it. He sensed a lot of passion there, barely restrained, though directed at who or what he couldn't tell. He was tempted to pull the photo of the young Van Der Meer out of his pocket and show it to her just to gauge her reaction. But he restrained himself. There would come a time for that but now it would be a distraction.

"Perhaps I simply feel safer with my own protection. That's certainly not a crime, is it?" she asked defiantly.

"No, of course not, but…"

"Is this an official interrogation? Am I now a suspect?" Van Der Meer had now seized control of the interview. "Because if it is, I'll need to have my lawyer present."

"No, it's not an interrogation, yet. We don't consider you a formal suspect, merely a person of interest who has a lot of information that is material to our investigation." Berté attempted to regain the initiative. "However, I must ask you, what are you afraid of, ma'am? Has someone in the hotel threatened you? Do you fear you'll be the next victim?"

Apparently, his attack struck a nerve. Van Der Meer remained silent for a moment and looked down at her lap briefly as if to compose herself. When she looked up again, her eyes were even sharper and more intent than before. "I could be, yes."

"So you believe the murder had something to do with you. Do you think you were the intended victim?"

Once again composed, Van Der Meer raised her shoulders with graceful indifference. "I don't know. I believe figuring that out is your job. And while you're doing that, I'm seeking to protect myself, nothing more."

"And you have no intention of helping me do that job do you, *ma'am*?" He deliberately emphasized the word "ma'am" in an attempt to rattle her.

Van Der Meer ignored his effort. "I will tell you what I know, but if you think that I am somehow responsible for this horror, you are seriously mistaken."

There was a ring of steel in Van Der Meer's voice that contrasted with her angelic appearance.

As Berté's involuntary sigh filled the room, Parodi stirred in his seat, producing an annoying creak.

"You had a motive," said Berté, ignoring Parodi.

"Me?"

"Yes. Do you deny your relationship with Sommariva? Do you deny having a jealous argument with him just a few days ago?"

Van Der Meer jumped up from her chair. "Who… Who told you this… This…"

"This fact, ma'am?"

Van Der Meer turned her back on him and remained silent for a few seconds. "You're treating me like the prime suspect…" she said contemptuously before breaking out in laughter.

"Following your, ahh, reasoning," continued Van Der Meer moving across the room, "I killed Roberto and Ornella out of jealousy, and I decided to do it right here, in what is effectively my home. Actually," she smiled grimly, "now that I think about it, that theory might make sense to an amateur detective. It's true that Roberto and I were in a relationship. We tried to be discrete, but it wasn't really a secret. And I suppose that some gossiping maid told you that one evening I had a quarrel with him and I got slightly carried away. On the other hand, my distrust of him was not misplaced as we now know all too graphically." She stopped for a moment, taking in a deep breath and forcibly swallowing the lump in her throat. "But from that to killing them! If you accuse me, you're a discredit to your profession, neither a good psychologist nor a good detective." she taunted. "You don't understand what motivates your suspects. You don't have concrete evidence of guilt – certainly not of my guilt or you would have arrested me."

She's right. What would the great Inspector De Vincenzi have thought of you?

'She is thinking aloud,' Berté thought, while the countess stared him down with an equal mixture of defiance and pain. Berté remembered the ex-secretary's words: the countess appeared controlled, but inside she was suffering. She must have loved Sommariva. She hid it well, but it could not escape Berté's attentive eye. A mature love, but one that could be dangerous for all that, as Berté knew from experience. It was also a love in which they were not equals and in which Van Der Meer had the upper hand, at least economically.

"Are you alright, Inspector?" Van Der Meer asked, her look of defiance shifting to concern.

Berté brought himself back to the present with a sharp intake of breath. "Signora Van Der Meer, I am sorry that you have such a negative opinion of me," he said, shaking his head. "I seek the truth. Perhaps I am clumsy and ill prepared, but what I lack in psychological insight I make up for with dogged persistence. I don't give up and, sooner or later, I'll find who murdered Sommariva and Ferrari. And during that process, I'll also discover why you're so afraid."

The countess's gaze hardened but Berté continued, undaunted.

"You're very afraid, but you don't trust me. You're taking a big risk not confiding in me. And you may also be preventing a killer from being brought to justice." He continued to stare at her intensely, but the countess neither lowered her gaze nor spoke.

"Well… I'll say goodbye, then," concluded Berté, turning and leaving the room without another word. He nodded distractedly to the guard as he passed through the door followed by Parodi. As they walked to the elevator, a waiter passed them pushing a cart with what was apparently Van Der Meer's lunch. Berté saw him stop in front of the countess's room where the bodyguard checked the contents and entered the room behind the waiter.

"Something about that woman doesn't smell right." commented Parodi as they entered the elevator.

"You're right. I don't know why, but there is something about her that doesn't ring true. You can tell that she is grieving for the death of her employees. And yet, she's always perfectly put together, impeccably dressed… And above all, perfectly in control, even when she's not. She keeps her cards close, that one."

"You know what I thought of, Sir?" asked Parodi. "An old movie, *Sunset Boulevard*. Do you remember it?"

Novels, songs, newspaper articles, movies… This was certainly a multimedia murder. It seemed to trigger memories and associations in everyone, even the staunchly business-like Parodi. As it happened, Berté remembered that movie well. He had a brief vision of an old actress with heavy makeup and spirited eyes whose name he couldn't remember, alongside an intriguing William Holden. It was a movie his father often quoted and one of his mother's favorites.

"It's about a mature silent movie actress who shoots her young lover," continued Parodi. "I have to ask: if someone a bit long in the tooth like the countess manages to have someone like Sommariva as a lover, why would she kill him? Would it really be just because he took a little detour with a secretary? Van Der Meer seems like an intelligent and rational woman, I don't see her as someone who goes off on a murder spree in a fit of jealousy… Well, I could be wrong, but I really can't imagine it… In any case, where would she have gotten a hold of the gun?"

Berté thought about it for a moment. Parodi's logic was not to be underestimated. Sometimes people follow unlikely tangents when the truth is much simpler.

"Van Der Meer knows how to shoot," he answered. "I found out this morning. Both she and her husband – and her stepdaughter as well – regularly entered shooting competitions. She has trophies. So she handles weapons and probably even owns some."

"Irrelevant," snorted Parodi. "Our murder weapon wasn't used in any competition. It's an illegal weapon with a silencer and no markings. She didn't have this lying around her hotel room. It was acquired specifically for this hit. And it's not something you can pick up on Amazon. So where – and how – did she get it?" Parodi lowered his voice as Gianasio passed by, talking with one of her officers. Berté caught Parodi's annoyed look and smiled to himself. Parodi was extremely loyal to people he liked – and people he didn't.

"You know, Parodi," he said, deciding to throw his sergeant a bone, "I think we need to dig into Sommariva's soul. We need to know what he really felt about Van Der Meer. Was it love? Did he exploit her or did he really care for her? I know this is going to be a tough assignment and that delving so deeply into the emotional side of things is a little outside of normal police work, but no one else on the team has the right blend of perspective and ability. Will you do it?"

Shameless. Utterly shameless.

Parodi stood a little taller, his face a study in pride and satisfaction. "Very well, Sir. I'll start working on it right away. I have a couple of hotel guests, friends of the countess, that I want to talk to... If my mother is anything to go by, these women are a bit bored and dying to gossip, especially to a police officer in the middle of an investigation. Let me see what I can turn up." With that, Parodi made a beeline for a table of well-dressed older women playing cards.

Berté's smile of satisfaction was interrupted by his vibrating phone. It was at text from Patty. He was tempted to not read it, but curiosity got the better of him.

'So now you're "investigating" young blondes? I saw your photo in *Il Secolo XIX*. Liar, liar, liar! This time you're not getting away with it! I never want to see you again!'

Berté began to laugh. He couldn't help himself. Not many things were certain in life but Patty's fixation was certainly one of them. Once she had determined what she wanted, she just wouldn't let it go. And in this case, what she wanted was him. It was flattering, really, being inexorably pursued by a beautiful woman. He couldn't deny it gave him a certain thrill.

As does adultery.

Berté stifled an ironic smile. Touché, you Bastard.

He saw Sabatini approaching, followed by a tall and robust man he recognized as Ferrari's ex-boyfriend, Antonio Brioschi.

Brioschi had red, swollen eyes and a frightened expression that seemed out of place with his athletic physique. His hair, which he wore almost to his shoulders, was greasy and unkempt. A broken man, Berté thought, and also an alcoholic, if his breath was anything to go by.

"Come, Signor Brioschi," Berté invited him, "follow me."

The man followed Berté into the "Torture Chamber" where they both sat.

"So, you were Ornella Ferrari's boyfriend…"

Brioschi broke down, crying like a child and hiding his face in his hands. Berté remained silent, looking away from him and beckoning Sabatini to pour him a glass of water.

"Sorry, Inspector," said Brioschi after drying his eyes and refusing the water, "but when I learned of Ornella's death I was beside myself… I can't believe what happened."

"When did you see her last?"

"I arrived here on Saturday… She had called me and asked to talk."

"Did she tell you she was having problems, that things were not going well with Signora Van Der Meer?

"No… No, she wanted to talk about our relationship… She wanted us to get back together."

Berté let out a huff of impatience, smacking the table with the papers that Parodi had brought him. These papers were not just for show and contained a lot of useful information on the person in front of him.

"Brioschi, I am going to say this once. Telling lies will get you nothing but trouble. Would you like to start again?" Berté's voice had taken on a flat, menacing tone that was even more disconcerting than an angry one would have been.

The man let out a small gasp. "I, I don't know what you mean, I…"

"You think that the police are all idiots? You think I'm an idiot? Stop lying and tell me the truth!" Berté's command rang across the room.

Sabatini sat very still, his gaze fixed in front of him. But had the unfortunate Brioschi had an iota of attention to spare for him, it would have been instantly clear that he was struggling not to laugh. Sabatini was well acquainted with his boss and his methods.

"But no, no, I…" stammered Brioschi.

"You exchanged dozens of text messages with Ornella. Do you think we haven't searched her phone and read them?" With that, Berté fanned out the stack of papers he had been holding to reveal printed transcripts of the chats pulled off Ornella Ferrari's phone.

A flash of abject fear passed through Brioschi's eyes and his resistance collapsed. "I came here to beg her to come back to me," he said as Berté nodded, "but she wanted nothing to do with me."

"Did she tell you that she was in another relationship?"

"No. I tried to press her about that but she denied it. She told me she had no feelings for me anymore and that we were done." He pronounced the last words with obvious pain.

"And after your lively conversation in that bar downtown…" he stopped, waiting for Brioschi to nod "you didn't see her again?"

Brioschi hesitated, then he said: "No, not exactly. I got a room at the Pensione Gli Ulivi in town. I was determined to see her again. But…"

So far so good, thought Berté, this matched the text messages they had found.

"The 'but' is that Easter day you came here to the Grand Hotel Miramare to look for her. And that same night Ornella was murdered."

"I called her from the reception, but she refused to see me." Brioschi squealed. "I wouldn't take no for an answer… If she had been willing to see me, perhaps she would still be alive! I wanted to bring her back to Turin with me, why didn't she listen to me?" Brioschi began sobbing again.

"When and how did you find out that Ferrari was killed?"

"Only yesterday afternoon, on the television."

"The morning after the murder, however, there aren't any text messages from you to the victim. Why didn't you send her any?"

Brioschi jumped out of his seat, his face turning purple. "You think I killed her? No, no, no… I want a lawyer!" he shouted.

"Sit down!" Berté ordered. "You've been watching too many American movies. That's not the way it works here. If we conclude you are implicated, we'll bring you in for formal questioning and then you'll have all the lawyers you can handle. In the meantime, especially if you aren't guilty of anything, just tell us the truth and you'll be fine. But if you refuse to cooperate we'll charge you with *favoreggiamento*, aiding and abetting. Now, what did you do on Easter Sunday?"

Brioschi went from purple to pale and swallowed hard. "I slept in that morning because I drank a lot the night before. That afternoon I came here to find Ornella, then… well, I'm not too clear on exactly what happened after that, to be honest. But I know I didn't kill anybody!"

"I know that you were drinking at the hotel bar."

"Yes, yes…" he broke out in tears again.

Berté sighed. He could understand Brioschi's suffering but he couldn't absolve him. And he had a job to do. "Where were you that night between 10:00 p.m. and 1:00 a.m.?" he barked.

"I was in bed, sleeping it off!"

"Can anyone corroborate that?"

"No… I don't know. Maybe someone at the pensione saw me come in."

"How did you get to Lungariva? By car?"

"No, by train."

"Right. And a good thing, too. I know you lost your driver's license for driving under the influence. Do you have a firearms license?"

"Yes, but…"

"Good, as you can see, we know all about you, and when you want to, you can tell the truth. Go on like this, and you won't need a lawyer. We're done here, for now. But don't go anywhere. We'll be talking to you again."

Berté stood to signify that the interview was over.

"Look, Inspector, I didn't kill Ornella, I truly loved her… She left me because I drank, but I had decided to start rehab, I had come to tell her that…" Despite his demand for a lawyer just moments before, Brioschi was now refusing to shut up. Sabatini had to take him by the arm and lead him from the room, his teary protestations of love trailing behind him.

Berté watched him leave, suppressing an urge to roll his eyes. What a mess! A love sick, mourning alcoholic… with no alibi.

"Listen, Sabatini," he said when his officer returned, "we need to do a little more digging on Brioschi. I'll talk with Grossi, perhaps we have enough to have his clothes checked for residue and inspect his room…"

"Sounds good, Sir" responded Sabatini as he left.

If he was the murderer, Berté mused, his motive was very clear. However, pulling off the murder itself presented some practical difficulties. Brioschi, a desperate and abandoned alcoholic, who has nothing to lose and wants revenge, procures a gun. Unlike in Van De Meer's case, it was easy to imagine Brioschi doing that. He goes to the hotel to find the woman who has spurned him but she refuses to even see him. So he pretends to leave the hotel and instead wanders through the hallways – with nobody noticing him – hoping to meet her. He doesn't find her but, instead, discovers that she's visiting her new lover in his room.

How exactly does that work? Did he wait all night outside her room? Or his? To top it all off, by a random stroke of luck, he either steals or finds a hotel master key. Then, still unnoticed, makes his way up to Sommariva's room, opens the door, and kills Sommariva and Ferrari. He then sneaks downstairs and out the service entrance without anybody noticing him.

'It's an improbable scenario,' mused Berté, slipping a hand in his pocket, 'On the other hand, this case is full of improbabilities that we know have actually happened. Facts that actually happened. What's a few more?'

He took out the photo of the young Van Der Meer, stolen from Ferrari's aunt. He stared at it, trying to understand why it had piqued his interest. He had taken it in response to an instinct, but now was the time to make use of modern technology. He called Parodi and told him he was going to eat something and then return to his office at the station where he intended to spend the afternoon. He needed to take a walk and think.

The wind had strengthened, and the sea was dotted with sailboats. His mind went back to a Milanese engineer named Conte who owned a small sailboat he kept docked in Lungariva. Berté had met him when he had come into the station to report the theft of his wallet. As they were talking, Conte expressed his annoyance with owing a boat but never being able to take it out. His wife, it seemed, didn't want him to sail alone – a wise precaution as he grudgingly admitted – but he could never find anyone in Lungariva to sail with.

In the end, Berté and Conte had exchanged phone numbers and agreed they would go sailing together as soon as it could be arranged. The engineer had left the station with a smile, despite having lost his wallet and everything it contained.

Brilliant police work. Really first class.

Now the wind had picked up and it was perfect sailing weather, but Berté was not in any position to take the afternoon off, even though getting out on the water might have been just the thing to clear out his thoughts. If Grossi found out he'd spent the day tootling around in a sailboat, his desk would have been cleared out, too.

He found himself, by chance, but perhaps not entirely, in the arcade where the Passalacqua bakery, a Lungariva favorite, was located. Why resist an unhealthy temptation? After all, it was lunchtime and even police officers need to eat. To think is to act and Berté found himself in the shop and at the end of a line of patrons. The counter employees were cutting and serving the bakery's specialty, focaccia, with surprising speed and agility in a sort of breadknife ballet. As it was, he had just enough time to give due consideration to his choice. He eventually settled on a slightly underdone piece with extra olive oil and salt.

Proper focaccia is a Ligurian delicacy. Each bakery has its own house style and true connoisseurs appreciate their subtle differences. Some people argued whether Passalacqua's softer and more oil-rich focaccia is better than Pedemonti's crispier, crunchier focaccia. This is foolish. Is a well-aged Brunello better than a good champagne? Each one is perfect in its own way. In any case, his choice hit the spot and was exactly what he wanted at the moment.

Whether it was the exercise, the fresh air, or the focaccia, he now seemed to be thinking better. As soon as he entered the police station he went to find Belli who was working diligently at her computer.

"Francesca, how are you?" he asked the officer giving her a friendly pat on the shoulder.

"It's been a long couple of days but I'm hanging in there, Sir. I'm working on that chart you requested that summarizes the locations and the alibis for all the guests on the night of the murder."

"Excellent. I'll be in my office here in the station all afternoon if you need me for anything. Parodi and Sabatini are still at the Grand Hotel, along with some other officers from the Genoa squad. I believe forensics is done."

"Yes, I just heard from Parodi. Now it's up to the laboratory and the coroner. Pity about the weapon. We're not having any luck in tracing either the seller or the buyer, which is no surprise. The murderer probably left it there because they were sure that we wouldn't get anything out of it."

Berté sighed and holed up in his office. Luckily, apart from his double murder, the station was handling nothing but routine stuff that didn't really require his attention. He dialed the prosecutor's number and updated Grossi on the various leads that he was following. Then he pitched him on searching Brioschi's room and testing his clothes. Grossi demurred, however. He wanted to question Brioschi himself first.

Berté decided to make one final call.

"Marzia, let me take you somewhere nice for dinner tonight."

"Why don't we eat dinner here at my place instead? Now that we have a bit of time to ourselves, we can really talk about things."

Berté mentally pinched himself. Until that moment, Marzia hadn't been willing to talk about their relationship. Just the fact that she had proposed it to him made him happy.

Perhaps having her husband at home crimped her love life. These things happen.

Then she startled him with another question.

"After you're done with this case, will you be writing another story?"

"You still haven't told me what you thought of the first one I gave you."

"I want to do it when we have some time to really discuss it. But I will say that I found it moving. And you know what I think about things like this. If you really enjoy doing something, you should do it. Remember when I sang that song to you at Villa Danielli? That broke my 'singing block.' And now I sing all the time. Well, at least in the shower!" The image of the Rubenesque Marzia belting out love songs in the shower was too distracting so he pushed it from his mind. "Well, I'm glad I was useful for something."

"And much more. You have been very… liberating."

There was an awkward silence as both realized this wasn't really the time or the place. So they promised to meet for dinner and said goodbye. Berté decided to give himself a little break and do some writing. After all, even busy police officers can't be begrudged a little leisure time.

*****

Time fled and before Berté knew it, almost an hour had passed. He saved the file with a sigh. There must be something wrong with him. Where did he come up with these odd and twisted ideas? He discarded the obvious answer that his profession was the true cause of his passion for writing. He had done a search on the internet and discovered that many police officers wrote, and not just mysteries or thrillers. Among noir authors, it was easy to find crime journalists, prosecutors, psychiatrists, criminologists, true connoisseurs of the subject. One recent book by his friend, Andreone Corvi, delved into the secrets of famous mystery authors. Berté had devoured it, but among the interviews with great authors he hadn't found anyone who wrote stories in a fit of rage after being confronted by a murder victim.

He looked at his watch: it was only 4 p.m. Several hours remained until his dinner with Marzia. He now felt a little guilty for indulging himself so he vowed to spend those hours productively. He got up and went in search of Belli who he found glued to her computer monitor.

"Any news, Francesca?"

"I'm almost done with the chart you wanted, Sir."

"When you're done with that, I've got something else for you." He pulled out the photo he had liberated from Ornella Ferrari's aunt and dropped it on Belli's desk.

Belli picked it up and examined it. "This could take awhile," she observed. "This photo must have been taken in the 1950s. If it's OK with you, Sir, I'll keep working here until eight. Then I'll go home and have something to eat and a shower. I should be back here by ten at the latest."

Berté felt a pang of guilt. While he was planning an intimate dinner, his officers were working around the clock. He thought of those American TV shows where police officers got in lengthy chases and fistfights and wrapped up the most complicated cases within an hour, and all without messing up their hair.

One must allow for poetic license in fiction.

Yes, fiction! Real life isn't like that. Real police officers get tired, get sick, end up in hospitals and make mistakes, especially when they're exhausted.

"Sounds good, Francesca. But make sure you get some sleep tonight. And make sure nobody else in Lungariva sees this photo. You'll have to send it out to the police in her hometown, of course, and you should also send it to all the stations in Friuli. But ask them to be discrete. And I want to know as much as possible about Van Der Meer's past. Make this your top priority."

"Yes, Sir. I'll get on it tonight." Belli flashed him a broad smile which Berté returned before heading back to his office.

He didn't feel like returning to the Grand Hotel. Plus, he had to read several reports and prepare one of his own. He sat at his desk and worked for over an hour, before receiving a call from Gianasio, who was heading to Genoa for the autopsy. She had called Count Van Der Meer's daughter, who made a very good impression on her, but had nothing interesting to relate. Christine Van Der Meer was fond of her stepmother and she considered her a good and intelligent woman, with whom her father had been deeply in love. No problems concerning the inheritance had arisen between them after the Count's death. The will was precise, fair, and satisfactory to both parties. Christine had met Sommariva, but she couldn't say anything in particular about him. He seemed like a good professional to her, loyal to the lady for whom he worked. Berté and Gianasio chatted briefly about the next steps in the investigation and agreed to meet the next morning.

Deputy Assistant Chief of Police Berté was worried. By now they had taken statements from almost all the Grand Hotel's guests and employees. They were now entering that dangerous tunnel in which investigations get stuck. There were leads, yes, but they were missing evidence. No footprints or DNA, no eye witnesses… And plenty of suspects but no prime suspect. To take the next step, they needed hard evidence, not just plausible theories. And he didn't have any.

Van Der Meer was scared, but wasn't talking. Everyone spoke well of her and there appeared to be nothing to blemish her character. Was the motive tied to her wealth? Berté picked up the folder that contained the reports from his men on what was found in Sommariva's office. Van Der Meer's holdings were unquestionably extensive. Numerous bank accounts, two diamond mines, real estate in South Africa and in Europe. In Monte Carlo, for example, the woman owned an entire apartment building; in the Emilia Romagna region, a textile company. He got tired just reading the list of her assets, but he paused to study several of the corresponding documents, hoping to find anything suspicious.

But no luck. She paid lots of taxes, although, considering all her charitable donations, she could easily have paid less.

Now that's *suspicious!*

'It's a welcome sight,' thought Berté, ignoring the Bastard. 'Italy would be a different country if everyone did the same!'

He couldn't quite work out what he thought of Van Der Meer. He didn't think he liked her, but he knew he respected her. None of the documents he examined revealed any traces of wrongdoing, as far as he could tell. Berté read the report of the officer who had examined the contents of the computer found in Sommariva's room. There, too, nothing out of the ordinary. Either Sommariva was really good at hiding irregularities, or there weren't any. Where did all those assets come from? What was inherited from Count Victor and how much was the countess's personal property before the marriage? Her South African husband's inheritance was certainly large, Berté thought, but the ex-secretary Ferrari's testimony indicated that Van Der Meer was already wealthy before getting married. What was her maiden name again? He checked: Licia Trevisan. Something was niggling at the back of his mind, something that someone had said. He said to himself that the hand of God would reveal it to him in time. The hand of God? Now that was an odd image for him to conjure up. The hand of God... Oh well, his subconscious was like that sometimes. It would come to him eventually.

Ferrari said she had travelled frequently before settling down in South Africa with her husband. But to travel in the style that Van Der Meer did require a significant amount of money, Berté thought. And now he recalled that Ferrari had explained that Van Der Meer's first husband was a wealthy man and after his death she spent time traveling the world before ending up in South Africa. Suppose she was a gold digger, an adventuress intent on extorting money from elderly husbands using her charm and good looks?

The count's daughter had confirmed to Gianasio that her father had died of cancer in a prestigious South African private clinic where he had been treated for months.

'Gianna Ferrari had said the same thing, but I suppose we should investigate it further,' Berté made a mental note. And Van Der Meer was not the only person to investigate…

Her travels reminded him of Sommariva's son. His sister didn't even know where he had ended up, or, apparently, that he had reconnected with their father. Perhaps, when the son returned from India, he was in need of money, so he demanded it from his father and threatened him. Sommariva was adamant in denying him help and he retaliated by shooting him in a room with his occasional lover, hoping for an inheritance… Over the phone, Gianasio had told Berté she had tracked him down and would be bringing him in for questioning the following day. Berté was looking forward to what was sure to be an… interesting interview.

And what about the gambling bartender? In this case, perhaps eliminating the lender also eliminated the debt.

And Ferrari's ex boyfriend? He was an abusive man and an alcoholic, and they had argued violently.

Further back in the running, there were a number of elderly hotel guests deeply smitten with the beautiful countess and her blue eyes. Even a slight case of senile dementia erodes a person's control and can provoke rash acts. Who knows? Perhaps eliminating the handsome Sommariva, who was also betraying his employer, was someone's way of proving their devotion. That stiff colonel and his weapons, for example…Well, maybe, but…

Berté had too many theories and not enough evidence. That was the most upsetting aspect of this case. It appeared to be the perfect crime.

Berté looked at his watch: it was already nearly 8 pm. Belli came in to say goodbye and to tell him that she had started looking into the photo of the young Van Der Meer. She'd managed to establish that the *Augustus* was a ship of the Italia Line, a company that was a big player in transatlantic passenger ships before they were killed off by the airplane. From what she could tell, the photo was probably taken in the late 1950s. She hadn't been able to turn up a passenger manifest, though. Even Google doesn't know everything. She promised, however, that she'd resume the search first thing in the morning. Perhaps she'd try and track down the Italia Line, or whatever was left of it, and see if they still had their old records.

As Belli left his office, Berté mused that perhaps he should just show the photo to the countess and ask her about it. But he was certain, somehow, that he would get nothing. It would be better to wait. He turned on the small TV in his office and watched the evening news. There were shots of the Grand Hotel Miramare – a nice advertisement, nothing says luxury like a murder investigation – from all angles, and several interviews – one with Gianasio, who managed to be charmingly evasive. Fortunately for him, journalists had left him in peace. The local television reporters knew they ambushed him at their own risk, and it was just as well. He was convinced that the less information about the details of the murders given to the press, the better it was for the investigation. He had never liked the Orwellian "Big Brother" aspect of the media. Anyway, considering the presence of the investigators from Genoa, it was clear that the press thought Lungariva's little police station and its chief were small fry and not worth the effort. Berté wasn't complaining. It was better this way.

He called Parodi at the Grand Hotel and began by teasing him about his long stay there and asking if he wanted his mail forwarded. But Parodi had little to report. After hours of chatting with the elderly ladies who were wintering at the Miramare, he had picked up little other than useless gossip and tips on the best hair salon in the Riviera.

At 8:45 p.m. Berté stood up from his desk, stretched, put on his coat and left. The case was important, sure, but so was his life, he thought, while walking towards the Pensione Aurora. The sky was dark and the air was cold and humid. On the gentle breeze, he caught the smell of seawater, the smell of ancient stonework, the smell of Liguria. As he walked through the narrow *caruggi* and under the stone archways, he could see that the streets were empty and the restaurants were full. Everyone was sitting at their dining tables.

Like all the Italian Riviera, Lungariva was a prime tourist

destination, even this early in the year. After the war, it had been mostly Americans. Now, there were more and more people from various countries in Asia in the mix. And Asians loved luxury brands almost as much as Italians did. Lungariva had no shortage of luxury stores and Patty's first thoughts when she found out about his move to Lungariva were about all the shopping opportunities available there. By then they had already more-or-less broken up… And luckily, there was no possibility that she would decide to join him in Liguria.

The gulf, the houses with peeling walls that would be a crime to repaint, the narrow and dark *caruggi* packed with stores of every kind, the small harbor which left the charm of the old fishing village untouched… Lungariva was a charming place and he was beginning to love it.

'Italians are spoiled. Surrounded by so much beauty and they don't even see it, much less appreciate it.' he thought.

A cliché.

Yes, a cliché, but clichés come from somewhere. He, himself, had often complained about his exile to Lungariva.

And this surprises you? You're never happy about anything.

The teeming cafes and restaurants reminded him that he had not eaten since his slice of focaccia at lunch. His problems always seemed more dire when he was hungry. But he consciously put away his problems with the case and concentrated on his upcoming dinner with Marzia. During the Christmas holidays he had gone to Milan, or better, he had escaped to Milan, to avoid seeing her with her husband, and also for the trial on the death of his friend Valerio Brivio. They had solved the case, but there had been consequences, consequences that were still playing out, and so he returned frequently to the city. In a moment of weakness, he had even ended up in bed with Patty.

Talk about consequences.

The months since Christmas had been torture. He had never been alone with Marzia and had to put up with the constant presence of Pestarino, always clinging to her and monopolizing her attention.

Quelle surprise. Husbands are funny like that.

But things would be different now… Wouldn't they?

He opened the door of the Pensione Aurora with excitement.

Marzia wasn't in the now-empty dining room where Giustina was bussing tables. The waitress turned and gave him an angry glare: He was always the last one to arrive for dinner.

Have you been stood up?

Berté clenched his fist in anger, but before he could form a mental reply, he caught the smell of Marzia's perfume.

"The Deputy Assistant Chief of Police Berté is always late!" she said, entering the room. "Giustina, you can go, I'll take care of our guest myself," she chirped.

The waitress finished her work while Berté sat at the table and began flipping through the newspapers. It was fair that Marzia wanted to preserve appearances by addressing him formally in front of the waitress, but this small pretense bothered him nonetheless. He couldn't really picture himself playing the role of the clandestine lover: He despised affairs and sneaking around.

Perhaps you and the countess have more in common than you think.

Even Marzia's simple lie annoyed him.

Good one, Pinocchio!

Berté ignored the Bastard. True, he was sometimes obliged to tell lies in his line of work… and, he supposed, he wasn't above the occasional little white lie in his personal life… but what really mattered was being sincere in your heart and being able to look at yourself in the mirror.

LOL.

It was only a moment before Marzia re-entered the dining room, smiling. She was wearing a black and flowing wool dress matched with sporty, but high-heeled black boots. Marzia also had an excellent sense of style and didn't rely on brand names or trends like Patty did.

"Now don't be that way, Luigi." she said, reading him perfectly. "I'm sorry to have put on a show with Giustina, but you know, I have to be careful around the staff. Come along. Dinner is waiting for us in my apartment."

In all these months he had never entered Marzia's apartment, which was attached to the pensione. He hesitated briefly and then followed her. It seemed, somehow, indecent to make himself comfortable in Pestarino's house before his sheets were cold.

"I know what you're thinking," Marzia said to him, leading the way, "but please, don't feel like an intruder. Consider yourself just a friend that I'm inviting to dinner. Hotel owners do have homes of their own."

'A friend?' Berté thought, asking himself what game they were playing. They had been flirting for months, they made love, they called each other all the time, they wanted each other desperately, and now they were just friends? This was the first time he fell in love – yes, that was the correct word – with a married woman, and it was terrible. As a good southerner, he wanted his woman to be his alone. He didn't want to share her with a sea captain!

Marzia opened the door of the small apartment located on the ground floor of the pensione, and he entered, unable to utter a word, embarrassed and tense. The lights were dim, there were many scented candles on the wooden tables. The décor consisted of exotic furniture, rugs, mats and pillows that Pestarino had probably picked up during his travels. There was a long and comfortable white couch in front of a television mounted on an orange-toned wall. In the corner stood a refectory table set for two with a white tablecloth and white plates. There was also music playing. To Berté's surprise, it was dance music.

Marzia smiled. "Did you expect to be welcomed by an aria from *Nabucco*? I don't just listen to opera, you know. Too tragic. And tonight, I'm happy."

He drew her close and glued his mouth to hers, forgetting all his doubts and insecurities. It was a long and intense kiss. It was Marzia who wriggled out of his arms, and then brought two glasses from the table, filling them with white wine.

"Shall we toast?" she asked handing him a glass.

They drank and sat at the table.

Marzia had prepared stuffed vegetable appetizers, black olive paté on toasted rosemary bread, prosciutto, buffalo mozzarella cut in thin slices and topped with tomatoes and basil... Berté savored every bite, accompanying everything with a fresh and fruity Sauvignon. During the first course of vegetable lasagna garnished with small zucchini flowers, they talked of inconsequential things. As she served him a couple of slices of tender roast beef with a side of potatoes sautéed in butter and sage, Marzia said, "Look at the wine I found. A bottle of Curzio di Sante Marie di Vignoni. You once told me about it and I managed to get a hold of a couple of cases. You were right. It's excellent."

Berté was oddly touched. He had never been in a relationship where the other person actually listened to everything he said.

"Now let's talk about your short story," she said finally, while setting her wine glass on the table.

Berté nodded, while pouring himself another glass of Curzio. Given the subject, he thought it best to fortify himself.

"You know, it surprised me. I thought you wrote detective stories, given your work, and instead… You are more sensitive than I thought. And you really understood *Madame Butterfly* after listening to it for the first time with me."

Berté smiled what he hoped was a polite smile rather than a sickly one. If he were honest – which he definitely was not going to be in this case – he'd barely understood a word. But knowing it was one of her favorites, he'd studied the libretto on the internet before writing his story.

Well, as long as you're sincere in your heart!

"In any case," Marzia continued, fortunately ignoring his expression and serving him a piece of cake with Chantilly cream, "Your *Butterfly* is different from Puccini's. Yours hides a dark soul."

Berté decided to change the subject. "I'm happy that you liked the story, but now let's talk about us."

"Let me finish," Marzia told him, smiling and filling two small glasses of limoncello, "and then we'll talk about us."

Berté settled back into his seat with trepidation but Marzia had dropped the subject of opera.

"I think you should send your story to a publisher I know," she said. "His name is Stefano Servello. At the end of the books he publishes, he often includes a short story by an emerging author. Why not try?"

Berté emptied his glass of limoncello in a single gulp. "I've never let anyone read my stories," he said, pouring himself another and swallowing it in its turn.

What do you need the glass for? Why don't you drink it directly from the bottle?

"Servello could help you. If nothing else, I'm sure he'd have useful advice."

"I'll think about it, Marzia. But what about us?" Berté blurted out.

Well! I suppose you get points for directness, you romantic devil, you.

Marzia became unusually serious and paused to take a drink from her glass.

"Luigi, whatever you might think, I'm not the sort of woman to have an affair."

He grabbed her hand and held it tight. "I don't think of this as just an affair, Marzia. I think about you all the time, I want you, I desire you..."

"You think about me, you want me, you desire me, only because you don't really have me... Oh, don't look like that. It's perfectly normal. Be honest. If I told you I was going to leave Marco to be with you, would you come and live here, in this apartment? Would you forget about returning to Milan and taking up your rightful place? Sooner or later your involuntary exile will come to an end and you'll have to decide if you want to go back to Milan or remain here. I don't want to leave Lungariva. I like living here with my cats, my books, my flowers... I like running this pensione and cooking for my guests. I'm happy here."

"So? Are you telling me that *I'm* the one who's happy having an affair and sneaking around behind your husband's back? I admit I haven't really thought about the future... But I'm happy with you, and I want you only for myself. I'm crazy about you."

"What if I told you you already have me just for yourself?"

Berté stared at her blankly. "What do you mean? Are you going to tell me you aren't really married?"

"Not exactly. Marco is impotent." she said gravely.

Berté had been re-fortifying himself with another glass of limoncello and began coughing frantically.

"I've wanted to tell you for a while," continued Marzia, ignoring Berté. "But somehow it didn't seem right while he was still in the house."

"But how... when...?" Berté asked hoarsely. As many times as he had imagined having this conversation, it had never turned out quite like this.

"An accident, about three years ago. I'm not going into detail. But before you ask, the condition is permanent."

Berté just goggled at her, unsure of what to say.

"I've never talked about this with anyone," Marzia continued, her eyes lowered. "I've always been faithful to him. And he's always been very attached to me, but he's not stupid, and I'm still young… He offered to divorce me so I could have my life back, but I had my work and my passions. I didn't know what more I could want…" Marzia stopped talking and blushed.

Berté thought it must be his turn to talk but what was he supposed to say? Up until a few minutes ago, he would have been thrilled to hear that Pestarino had died in a fire. But now? He didn't know what to think.

What the hell is wrong with you? What do you mean you don't know what to think?

'But this changes things.' thought Berté.

Yes, it changes things. It makes them perfect. For God's sake, two minutes ago, you were whining that you didn't want to share her. And now you don't!

Berté remained silent.

Say something, you idiot!

For once, the Bastard seemed to have Berté's best interests at heart. But it was Marzia that broke the lengthening silence.

"I've shocked you, haven't I? I've been debating whether to tell you but I decided you had a right to know. I don't want you thinking I'm something I'm not."

"Yes, I'm shocked," Berté finally managed to say. "And I need to think about this…"

I take it back. Shut up.

Berté said nothing. He got up, quickly kissed Marzia, her eyes full of tears, and left.

The Third Day

He was surrounded by people demanding to talk to him, by ringing phones, and by hands waiving reports that required his signature. And his head was starting to pound. The day was not getting off to a good start.

He somehow managed to break free of the scrum and made a beeline for Belli's desk to see if she had made any progress with his stolen photo. He found her sitting at her station and talking on the phone while studying the screen in front of her. Berté caught her attention but she just shook her head. So still nothing on that front.

Berté slouched back to his office, took off his coat, and settled behind his desk. He'd had yet another sleepless night, in no small part because of his discussion with Marzia. He had finally fallen asleep just before dawn and then he had dreamed of… Pestarino. There was something seriously wrong with him.

You'll get no argument from me.

Not once, however, in all those long hours, had he thought about his double murder. To make matters worse, he had ignored the very first lesson his police detective father taught him when he heard he would join the police force. "Luigi," he had said to him while putting a hand on his shoulder, "when you become a detective – and I know you will – and are investigating a case, remember that justice is in your hands. You must commit yourself to that and everything else is secondary, your family, your friends, even your life. Don't let your personal problems distract you because if you won't see justice done, no one will." So Berté was not exactly covering himself with glory here. If he'd had the energy, he would have been deeply ashamed of himself. He stared into space, feeling drained, both physically and mentally.

Enough! He needed to put his feelings and his self-pity aside and focus on the investigation. There was a murderer to catch and his people were depending on him. His personal issues were going to have to wait. He turned on his computer and pulled up the scanned photo of Van Der Meer. He didn't know, exactly, what he hoped to get from that photo… Perhaps he should forget his fixation with her and start again. There was certainly no shortage of possible suspects. Perhaps the hand of God would guide him. Damn it! There it was again. Why must his miserable subconscious be so clever and enigmatic? Why couldn't he just have a prophetic dream or something? He took an Advil from his desk and opened a bottle of mineral water. Perhaps he could stop his headache before it started. At the least opportune moment possible, Belli burst into his office, waiving and shouting.

Berté began coughing and spilled a fair amount of the bottle on his shirt. It was a few seconds before he could focus on the papers that Belli was shoving in front of his face.

"Sir, look! Look at this! What do you see? This one is from Maniago, the town in the province of Pordenone where the countess claims she was born."

Berté examined what appeared to be a document issued to Licia Trevisan, born in Maniago on June 16th 1938, from Luciano Trevisan and Mariasilvana Pologrillo… Berté stared intently at the photo in the document's upper-left hand corner. Then he stared at Belli.

"Yes! Exactly!" Belli crowed. "Licia Trevisan is Van Der Meer's maiden name. But the young woman in your photo who we know as Van Der Meer is someone else. *Licia Trevisan is the girl standing next to her!*"

Berté again stared at the document and then at the picture on his screen.

'I knew it," he thought triumphantly. 'I just knew there was something about that woman that didn't ring true!'

But Belli wasn't finished. "Now look at these documents. After 1967, all of Licia Trevisan's documents have Van Der Meer's picture on them."

"You're joking."

"Not at all. Starting in 1967, Van Der Meer – or whoever she is – stole Licia Trevisan's identity. But, of course, she couldn't do anything about the documents the real Licia Trevisan had already filed in Maniago. And I have no information, yet, on what happened to the real Licia Trevisan."

Berté felt a rush of adrenaline, and all his worries seemed to vanish. He was definitely back in the hunt now.

"Let's find out who Van Der Meer really is," he said, jumping to his feet. "Find the passenger manifest for the *Augustus*. And see if we can get a hold of any immigration documents they might have on file for that trip."

"It's unlikely that's still available, especially the immigration documents. But I suppose we have to try. I've already contacted our embassy in Buenos Aires. I'm waiting for their response, but I only have this photo, and Van Der Meer has traveled the world… She was also married in South Africa using Licia Trevisan's documents. Sorting all this out is going to take time."

"Not necessarily. Van Der Meer can tell us all about it right now. Who's at the hotel this morning?" Berté asked holding his phone in his hand.

"Parodi."

Berté dialed. When Parodi answered, he ordered him to personally take charge of the countess and make sure she didn't leave the hotel until he got there. With that, he hung up without further explanation.

"Well, Francesca," Berté gloated, "if Van Der Meer speaks voluntarily, then we're golden. If not, we'll just have to back her into a corner. So pull out all the stops. Talk to everybody, in the passport office, in Maniago, in Pordenone, in Friuli… See if there is any way to get someone in Argentina and South Africa to cooperate. But we have to find out what happened to the real Licia Trevisan and who 'the countess' really is. This is our top priority. Whatever it takes, get to the bottom of this."

He put on his coat and ran out of his office calling for an officer to drive him to the Grand Hotel. He was just pulling up to his destination when his phone rang. It was Parodi.

"Sir, the countess is nowhere to be found, she's not in her room, she's not in the hotel. And her bodyguard is gone, too."

'Great. Just great,' thought Berté. 'How am I going to explain this to Grossi?' "Well, Sir, the good news is we've found the murderer. The bad news is that she walked away and disappeared from the hotel while we were guarding it." Shit. Where did they send you for punishment when you screwed up in a place like Lungariva?'

The minute the car stopped in front of the Grand Hotel, Berté leaped out and ran up the staircase that brought him to the lobby where both Parodi and the manager were waiting for him.

"Where the hell did she go? Did anyone see her leave?" Berté shouted, startling two hotel guests making their way to a late breakfast.

"The doorman says it was around 9:30. And she didn't walk. Her car is gone." Garaventa said in one breath, extremely pale, his face beaded with sweat.

"What car does she have?" Berté asked.

"A Bentley Continental Flying Spur in metallic blue."

"Do you have the license plate number?"

"I… I don't know. But reception will have it. We keep records of all the guests' cars if they park them on hotel grounds."

"Get it. Now."

The manager bowed jerkily and quickly turned away. Berté turned to Parodi. "We can't talk here. The interview room."

Once they had closed the door behind them, he continued, "Find that car. See if it's still in town. In a place like Lungariva, it isn't going to go unnoticed. If it's not, I want every officer between Rome and the Swiss border on the lookout for it. And call the bodyguard agency. Let's see if we can track him. Now bring me the maid… No, Parodi, I'm perfectly sane. Stop looking at me like that. I'll explain later."

"Sir, if I'm giving you the fish eye, it's not because I doubt your sanity. It's because last I checked there is only one of me and I can only do three things at once."

"Oh. Where's Gianasio?"

"I'm here," she said, pushing the door open. "What's happened?"

Berté briefly summarized recent developments.

"She's on the run. She must be guilty." offered Gianasio when he finished.

"We don't know that. Our killer may have gotten to her. There may even be an innocent explanation. It's not like she's escaped from custody. All we know right now is that she's left the hotel."

"Why are you defending her?" Gianasio exclaimed. "You don't find her behavior suspicious, especially given what we now know about her past?"

"Of course it's suspicious. And we need to find her immediately. I'm only saying that there's also the possibility that something has happened to her. We just don't know yet."

"Unlikely. She even has a bodyguard," said Gianasio. "Perhaps she's laying out on the beach working on her tan."

"This is not the moment for sarcasm. We need to find her. Apart from the risk to her safety, she's now our chief suspect and we've let her walk off under our very noses. Van Der Meer isn't the only one who's going to have to answer a lot of questions when Grossi finds out about this. Now go find that bodyguard!"

Gianasio pulled out her phone and walked to a quiet corner of the room. Berté passed a shaking hand through his disheveled hair, his heart pounding. But there was nothing for it now. He took out his phone and dialed Grossi's number. Berté quickly briefed him on their discoveries about Van Der Meer's past… and on how Van Der Meer had escaped.

The prosecutor was not amused. In fact, he was so angry that Berté entertained the brief hope that Grossi might be having a stroke – just a little one – and that would give him some time to fix this mess before it became completely unmanageable. But this was not turning out to be Berté's day. After repeatedly shouting about how incredibly incompetent it was for him to let her escape from a hotel full of police officers, he informed Berté that he was already in the car and would be arriving in person to continue their conversation.

Berté couldn't help but agree with Grossi's general assessment. If Van Der Meer really was guilty, he though bitterly, he had been played for a fool. And even if she weren't, he should never have let her simply disappear.

A frightened Consuelo, escorted by Parodi and the manager, entered the interview room and Berté sighed with relief. Finally something constructive to do!

"Where did Signora Van Der Meer go?" Berté asked her without preliminaries.

"I don't know. All I know is that this morning she told me she would be going out."

"At what time did she leave?"

"She had breakfast in her room at nine o'clock, and then she left."

"Did she take any luggage with her?"

"No."

"Are you telling the truth?"

Consuelo, clearly upset, was wringing her hands. "Yes. I'm telling the truth. I've worked here for ten years and the manager can vouch for me. I take care of her clothes and her suite but she doesn't confide in me. All I know is what I've already told you." With that, she burst into tears and covered her face with her apron.

Garaventa put a consoling hand on her shoulder. "Inspector, I know Consuelo well, she's honest and capable. I assigned her to take care of the countess specifically because I trust her. You can believe everything she tells you."

"All right, fine." Berté said quickly, "What did she take with her? If you've worked for her for two years, you should be able to tell us that, at least."

"She took her handbag, I don't know what, exactly, she had in it. She also took her beauty case. But that doesn't really count as luggage. She takes it with her everywhere."

"And her jewelry?"

"I don't know… Usually her jewelry is kept in the hotel safe."

Berté briefly considered whether he should ask the prosecutor about getting a search warrant for the safe but quickly put the idea aside. There were other priorities at the moment.

"Did the bodyguard have anything with him when he left? A suitcase, perhaps?"

"I don't know. I didn't see him leave."

At that moment Grossi made his entrance. Berté's finely-tuned detective skills allowed him to instantly deduce that the prosecutor was not happy. Parodi, who was no fool himself, grabbed Consuelo by the arm and escorted her away, leaving Berté on his own.

"She fooled us all, eh Berté? What a pity I talked you out of bringing her in!" the prosecutor commented sarcastically. His usual bonhomie had disappeared and his eyes were furious behind his thick glasses.

"Why do you say that?" Berté asked in return. He was equally furious, both at Van Der Meer and at himself, but he would rather be dragged into court than admit it.

"Because she's our murderer! You know damn well that's been my theory from the beginning though you couldn't see that yourself."

"And I still can't!" Berté retorted.

"Oh, come on! What does this blessed woman have to do to

convince you of her guilt? For God's sake, not only has she done a runner, she's stolen someone's identity and is operating under an alias!"

"Perhaps she's disappeared because she's afraid."

"Afraid? She had a personal bodyguard and lived in a hotel full of police officers. What is she afraid of? Who is she afraid of? And why?"

"Perhaps she fears something from her past."

"You mean like her various crimes catching up with her? Yeah, that could be." agreed the prosecutor sardonically.

Berté decided to cut the conversation short. He was still convinced that, whatever Van Der Meer might have done in the past, she wasn't their murderer. But he didn't want to try and explain his reasoning to Grossi since he hadn't fully explained it to himself. He still needed a lot of pieces to complete the puzzle. "She's not our murderer and I will find her. Now please let me get back to work!" Berté's tone was peremptory.

The prosecutor stared at him with bulging eyes. For a moment, Berté thought he was about to be removed from the case. But then Grossi's face cleared and he said, "All right. Have it your way. When you finally get this mess under control, you will explain to me what you have in mind, because it's obvious you do have something in mind. So get to it!"

Once Grossi had left, Berté took out his phone and called Belli.

"Francesca, any news?"

"No, Sir, I'm waiting for some more info on the photo. But I can tell you that our steamship *Augustus* departed in February of 1957 from Genoa, heading for Buenos Aires. I'm looking for the passenger list. No news of Licia Trevisan. I haven't turned up any death certificates matching that name, but all consulates have been notified."

"All right, Francesca. Keep up the good work." With that, Berté ended the call and paused to collect his thoughts. Where would she go? If she were fleeing the country, her most likely destination was Switzerland, though France was closer. But what if she was looking for a bolt hole close by? He checked his watch. Yes, she could have arrived in Varese Ligure by now. It was time for a call to Van Der Meer's devoted former secretary, Gianna Ferrari.

"Deputy Assistant Chief of Police Berté, here."

"Is there any news?" Ferrari's voice was filled with anxiety.

"Some. But I wouldn't say it's good news. Signora Van Der Meer left the hotel this morning and she's not answering her phone."

"Oh my! You don't think something happened to her?"

"We certainly hope not. Nonetheless, she may be in danger so it's critical that we speak to her as soon as possible. Have you heard from her?"

"No, no, not today." Ferrari's voice broke.

"Now listen carefully. This is very important. If she does contact you, you need to call me immediately. It's a matter of Signora Van Der Meer's safety. Do you still have the card I gave you?"

"Of course, of course."

"Another thing: you had mentioned that she had gotten married while she was in South America. I need you to tell me everything you know about her first husband."

"I don't know very much. Just that he was a wealthy South American, a rancher of some sort I think, who left her everything."

"What was his name? Do you have a photo? Do you remember anything else about him? Anything at all?"

"She never told me his name… And I never saw a photo. The countess mentioned him to me maybe twice, in passing. She hardly ever spoke about that period of her life. All I know is that when he died, she left Argentina and started to travel."

"When did he die?"

"I don't know."

"Did you ever see the signora's identity documents? Maybe a passport?"

"Of course! She was born in Maniago, a village in the Friuli region, but as far as I know she didn't have any relatives left there."

"Did she tell you why she left?"

"Not really. I know her parents died during the war and that she lived in a boarding school run by nuns. When she became an adult, she left for Argentina to try here luck there."

"Which nuns? Do you remember the name of the school? Was it in Maniago?"

"I don't know. Again, we never talked about it… The countess didn't talk much about her childhood, either. She did talk a lot about her second marriage and her years with Count Van Der Meer, however."

No surprise there, Berté thought. She was hiding something and her past – or at least her name – belonged to somebody else. The less said about all that, the better, especially if you were now a rich pillar of society and a countess.

"One more thing, Signora. You showed me a folder with some documents related to her charity work. I would like to examine them. I'll send someone to pick them up this afternoon."

"Certainly, Inspector, anything to help the countess."

Berté was finishing up his call with Ferrari just as Parodi entered the room.

"Sir, she took her handbag, ID documents, and credit cards. But no suitcase. It's possible she decided to leave everything behind and purchase whatever she needs along the way. She can certainly afford to."

"Where would you go, Parodi, if you left Lungariva on the run?"

"From here? I would go to France. It only takes two hours. Either that or to Switzerland. She could be in Lugano in three hours and she can access some of her bank accounts from there."

Berté nodded and dismissed him. Then he gave Belli another call, asking her to search through every convent boarding school in Friuli for traces of… their quarry. At this point, he didn't really know what to call her. Having handled everything on his to-do list and having a moment to spare, he resumed berating himself for his stupidity. Why didn't he properly interrogate her when he'd had the opportunity? One thing was for sure. If he did have another chance, he would not be intimidated by an aristocratic bearing and steely blue eyes. Berté sighed and made his way out of the interview room. In the lobby, he stopped to speak to Garaventa.

"We're missing something. We need to re-interview the staff. Can you provide me with a shift schedule?"

Garaventa stared back at him grimly. "I'd like to talk to you, Inspector," said the manager, his voice trembling slightly, "but not here in the lobby. Come to my office."

He led Berté to a very elegant room with wood paneled walls and a polished antique desk, inviting him to sit in a small armchair while he sat down across from him. The manager was embarrassed. He fiddled with the items on his desk and aligned already perfectly organized stacks of papers, sweating all the while. He cleared his throat a few times and finally spoke. "Inspector, perhaps this isn't the best time, as I know you're very busy, but I haven't slept in two nights... I need to explain this to you before someone..."

"Garaventa, don't waste my time. Tell me what you know."

The manager now looked both embarrassed and dismayed. "Ornella and I... were... I mean... It was really nothing serious..." he mumbled.

Berté slammed his fist on the desk, causing the manager to flinch. He simply could not tolerate people who beat, endlessly, around the bush, which was exactly what Garaventa was doing. Life was too short.

"Why didn't you tell me this sooner?" he barked.

Garaventa blushed and remained silent. Berté internally rolled his eyes and exhaled wearily. If he were in an old movie, he could have beaten the information out of him, which, he had to admit, was tempting. But nowadays, some diplomacy was called for. "Look," he said, trying to keep the annoyance out of his voice, "I'm not a marriage counselor. I'm not a priest. And I'm not your mother. Tell me everything you know. If it's got nothing to do with the case, that will be the end of it. But if you refuse to tell me and I decide you are intentionally obstructing my investigation..." He let the threat hang in the air.

"You're right," whimpered the manager, who was now nearly in tears, "I have nothing to do with the murder. Ornella and I... we had an affair. It was very brief. I broke it off because I couldn't bear being unfaithful. I haven't told my wife anything. In fact, I haven't discussed it with anyone. The only reason I'm telling you now is because, despite our best efforts to keep it a secret, someone in the hotel could have found out about it. I preferred that you heard the truth from me rather than from some hotel employee."

Berté remembered Parodi telling him about a threatening look that the manager had given the chef. Yes, indeed. Someone in the hotel did know about this affair.

"So you were having an affair with Ferrari. I assume that means you got to know her better than most. What can you tell me about her that I don't already know?"

"Well, I don't know what you already know so I don't know." The manager smiled grimly.

What a smartass.

Berté could only agree.

"But these are my impressions," Garaventa continued, "Ornella was very charismatic. You see, quite a few women pass through my hotel, but I've never… Well, she was different, I fell for her."

"There's a first time for everything."

"I assure you that for me it will also be the last…" The manager had recovered his confidence, his voice was much more relaxed. "We didn't really have a true relationship. We had dinner twice, and there was only one time that we…"

"I understand. Continue."

"Ornella wanted to settle down. She was looking for an opportunity to marry a rich man and live 'the good life.' She used to ask me for information on guests at the hotel – even the very old ones."

"Oh, really?"

"Yes. And what's more, I suspect that if I hadn't broken it off, she would have, because I wouldn't tell her anything."

"So you realized that the only reason she slept with you was to determine who the 'big fish' in the hotel were, so she could catch them in her net. Is that so?"

"In retrospect, yes, I was a real idiot for believing that she was interested in me. But again, I told her nothing. My guests have nothing to worry about. I am completely discreet. I don't discuss their business."

"Except with policemen?"

What the hell is wrong with you?!?

"Except with policemen." The manager was blushing again.

"Good for you. When did all this happen?"

"A couple of months ago, and, again, it was over very quickly."

"You didn't know that Ornella had an affair with Sommariva?

"No."

"And you never saw her trying to flirt with any of your wealthy clients?"

"Hard to say. I saw her talking with De Cillis a few times. He certainly met her criteria. But he's senile and his children keep an eye on him."

"So Ferrari was trying to marry him so she could enjoy his inheritance?"

"Maybe. She used to say that she wanted to follow in the countess's footsteps. Nothing happened with De Cillis, though. Of that I'm certain. He didn't like Ornella. I suppose, senile and all, he figured her out before I did."

Berté let out an involuntary chuckle. "She didn't tell you anything about Signora Van Der Meer?"

"I know that Ornella couldn't stand the countess. She used to call her 'the old woman.' She couldn't understand how her aunt had managed to spend so many years working for such a 'bitch'. Her words. Definitely not mine."

"So she really opened up to you…"

"Yes, she needed to vent, and she knew that I can keep a secret."

"So she planned on working for Van Der Meer only until she found the right chicken to pluck, is that what you think?"

"That's more or less it."

"Did she tell you anything about her ex?"

"Yes, she told me that he was still pursuing her, but that she didn't want anything to do with him and that he's a drunk."

"Is there anything else you should be telling me?"

"No."

"You're sure?"

Garaventa placed his hand on his heart. "I've told you everything… Can I count on you to keep this between us?"

"Let me be clear. If I find the murderer and you weren't involved, I'll do my best to keep this conversation to myself. But if this is not the case…"

"So it's possible this may come out in court." Garaventa had turned pale and gone back to sweating.

"Come now, don't stress yourself unnecessarily. If you've told me the truth you have nothing to worry about."

Garaventa stood up and offered Berté a trembling hand. "If my wife knew, she would be terribly hurt."

"I believe it. Nobody enjoys being cheated on."

After leaving Garaventa's office, Berté left the Grand Hotel and went directly to the police station for an update on the search for the countess. But first, he had to run a gauntlet of waiting reporters eager for news. Even his old nemesis Costa was there. As the opportunity was too good to miss, Berté approached him and sarcastically thanked him for the great service that he'd done by publishing his photo with Gianasio. But Costa was not in the least embarrassed and began to pepper him with questions. Berté declined to comment apart from graphically suggesting that Costa do something anatomically impossible.

Once he had made his way through the crowd and reached the safety of his office, he dropped into his chair, seething. His anger wasn't so much directed at Costa — who, Berté would have admitted in his calmer moments, was just doing his job — but Van Der Meer. What the hell was she thinking, playing him for a fool? Did she really imagine she could simply escape like that? She had refused to be open with Berté. And though she pretended to be cool and calm, he knew now for a fact that she was very afraid of something.

With a sigh, he checked his messages. There was nothing on the search so he could only assume that, so far, it had been unsuccessful. To make matters worse, there was a voice mail from Grossi, "It would be very much in your interest to find Van Der Meer immediately." Grossi was no longer shouting. His tone was matter-of-fact, almost friendly. Berté knew that what was left of his career stood on a knife edge. But short of wandering the streets of Lungariva shouting her name as if she were a lost dog, there was nothing else he could do at the moment. He could only wait for the search he had put in motion to bear fruit. For Berté, that could only mean one thing: It was time to eat.

He gathered his overcoat and, using a back entrance to avoid the scrum of journalists, he headed toward the harbor. Perhaps some fresh sea air would clear his head and give him an inspiration. As he neared the harbor, he caught a strong odor from the docks. Though it wasn't exactly what he'd had been hoping for, Berté didn't mind. At that moment, he wouldn't have wanted to be in Milan even if he could. Better the natural stench of rotting fish than the smell of diesel fumes and car exhaust. Better the sound of waves lapping against the breakwater than the sounds of traffic. In short, better tiny Lungariva, even with all its provincialism, than a teaming metropolis that didn't care if you lived or died. The authentic Milan, the Milan of his parents and his childhood, was a thing of the past. It only survived in the old songs sung in the small Teatro della Memoria, the Theater of Remembrance, on via Cucchiari. He went there once with his friend, Andreone, and he was moved to tears, listening to the old songs in dialect that his mother used to hum. If Van Der Meer's escape got him cashiered, he mused, perhaps he could become a fisherman. He would get hired on one of the fishing boats that unload their fish at Lungariva's market every evening at five. No murderers, no thieves, only the stink of fish, which would smell like roses compared to the corpses he had to deal with now. Perhaps even his relationship with Marzia would make sense.

The thought of calling Marzia flashed into his mind. But he made a great effort to stop himself. Then again, strategic silence was not his style either… And what would she think of his disappearance after her revelation? So he couldn't just disappear. But he didn't really know what he wanted to say. He opted for the comfortable ambiguity of a brief text.

'Case has gone crazy today. Talk soon.' That ought to do it. Not exactly poetry, but given his self-imposed limitations, probably the best he could hope for.

That done, he headed inland for a place with a little less sea air and better food. He eventually settled on a café and a grilled mozzarella and prosciutto *panino*. As there was still no word on the search, he decided on a walk along the beach. As he rambled, a dog with a piece of cardboard in its mouth came trotting towards him.

"Come here!"

The call came from the dog's owner. The dog, however, ignored the command. Dropping his prize, he began to enthusiastically jump at Berté and lick his hand.

The dog was a beagle. He was familiar with the breed, as one of his uncles, a seasoned hunter, had owned a few which he used to use to flush game. As a child, when he went to the countryside to visit, Berté would occupy himself by taking them around the meadows. He knelt down to scratch the dog under the chin and received a happy yelp in exchange.

"I'm so sorry. When he follows a trail he doesn't listen to anyone!" the dog's owner exclaimed, as she caught up with the now ecstatic beagle.

"There's no need to apologize." Berté reassured her. Despite the encounter in his office the day before, he loved dogs and this one was absolutely wonderful.

His owner put him back on his leash and resumed their walk. As they moved away, the woman said sternly, "No more of that. You behave yourself, Tango!"

Berté stopped dead in his tracks, staring slack-jawed. Tango. The hand of God. Maradona… Argentina! Yes. Argentina. That was the connection.

He was mentally berating his perverse subconscious – The hand of God. Really? – when his phone pinged. Marzia had texted him back. **"I'll wait for you… always."**

As reassuring as that was, now wasn't the time for sentimentality. He had to get his hands on the witness statements his officers had compiled from the hotel guests. Argentina. Ha! Rushing back to the Grand Hotel, he called Parodi and gave him his instructions. He still needed the details. But he was convinced that he was right and that there was something there.

What happened to the real Licia Trevisan? And what was the name of that tall blonde girl who smiled on the *Augustus*, and who was now a wealthy countess? What had happened in Argentina? There were Argentine guests and employees at the hotel. Was that a complete coincidence? Or did one of them have some connection to Van Der Meer's past? Berté again dialed Belli's number. She answered with a sort of sigh that meant 'I'm doing my absolute best. Do you think I'll go faster if you keep bothering me?'

"Any news?" he asked, not even knowing what he was hoping for.

"Depends on what you mean by 'news.' I can tell you that none of the convent schools that I've contacted in the Friuli region had any students by the name of Licia Trevisan. And these nuns know their business. They have all their records in order back to the 19th century. I even sent a photo of the young countess to see if that might help identify her. I'm still waiting for some of them to get back to me. A few have already responded. Some don't keep a photo archive."

"Any news about the ship?"

"I've got a lead on a passenger manifest for the *Augustus* but I haven't received it yet."

Berté thanked her and hung up. By then he had arrived at the Grand Hotel so he made his way to the interview room where Parodi was waiting. His heart was beating fast and a thousand thoughts cascaded through his head. He took a couple of deep breaths to calm himself. He would get one chance at this. He needed to think carefully about what questions to ask and what words to use. He sat down and perused the files Parodi stacked in front of him. "OK," he told Parodi, taking another deep breath, "bring in Gomez."

"You want to speak with me?" a tall man with a very strong accent now stood in front of Berté. The man was in his sixties, well built, with thick hair that was still black.

"You are signor…"

"Fernando Louis Gomez. But I do not…" The man looked around, confused.

"It's only a chat. Please sit down. We're talking to all of the hotel's guests."

"*Está bien.* But your colleague interviewed me before."

"I know, but I'd like to talk with you, too." Berté looked down at the record of the previous interrogation he had in front of him.

"So you're from Argentina?"

"*Sí*, I'm from Saladillo, but I live in Buenos Aires."

"Your family is from…" he invited him to answer with a wave of the hand.

"My father was *de origen español*, his parents came from Seville. My mother's family is from Argentina."

"What do you do for work?"

"I own some supermarkets."

"Why are you here?"

"A holiday. I come to Italy sometimes, but to Liguria, no. But I wanted to see Portofino, it's *muy famosa*… so *mi amigo*, who's opening an Argentine restaurant in Rapallo, invited me to visit. I spent Easter with him.

"Your Italian is very good. Why?"

Gomez laughed. "*En Argentina* I have many friends *de origen italiano.* Of course, everybody can speak Spanish, but half the country can speak Italian as well. It is useful for me since I come here frequently for work and as a tourist."

"Are you married?"

"No. Widowed."

"Do you have any children?"

"Sadly, no…."

"Did you ever sail on the MS *Augustus*?"

"On the what?" Gomez appeared surprised at the question and seemed to search his memory.

"On the MS *Augustus*, an ocean liner traveling between Italy and South America."

"No."

"On Easter Sunday, you say you were in Rapallo at your friend's house. Until what time?"

"Until 6 p.m. Then I returned to the hotel and relaxed in my room. It was a big lunch. Later that night, I went out for a walk. I got back to the hotel around 10 p.m. and spent an hour or so in the bar before I went to bed."

"Did anyone see you?"

"Inspector, *no entiendo*. I have explained all this already." The man seemed to be getting annoyed by the questions, and was fidgeting in his seat. Berté did not care.

"You left the hotel early the next day. Where did you go?"

"To Mass. In the church above the fish market. *Me gusta, es una iglesia hermosa. Talvez el padre se acuerda de mi…* That is to say, perhaps the priest will remember me. I was in the first pew. But *porqué esta* question?" Now there was no doubt that Fernando Gomez was annoyed.

"We're merely confirming our information. I'm asking all the hotel guests the same questions."

Gomez looked at him skeptically, but said nothing.

"Anyway, thank you for your cooperation. I think we have everything we need. Again, thank you for coming in." said Berté, smiling.

Gomez stood up and turned to go, but as he reached the door, Berté interjected "Oh yes! There was one other thing. How well do you know Signora Van Der Meer?"

Gomez turned slowly. "The blond Italian *señora*?"

Berté nodded. "Yes. The countess."

"Not at all, really. As I've told you, I've never been to Liguria before and don't really know anyone."

"Do you know a Licia Trevisan?"

The man stared at him defiantly. "I have never heard of this *señora* before."

Berté gave him a friendly nod and waved his hand to indicate that he could leave. Then he lowered his eyes to the useless notes that he'd pretended to take.

The moment the Argentine left the room shooting Berté one last worried look, Parodi squeezed his way through the door. It was clear from his face that he had something important to say and that Berté wasn't going to like it.

"Sir, we just got word from the station. The pensione where Ferrari's ex, Brioschi, is staying called 911 this morning. Brioschi didn't show up for breakfast and, after knocking for a bit, they entered his room with a master key. He was on the bed, unconscious. We don't have any toxicology reports yet but the paramedics think he overdosed on sleeping pills."

Berté sank into his chair with a hand over his face. He knew that man was on the edge of a cliff… He should have foreseen something like this. "Send Sabatini to the hospital and keep me informed. And send in the next person on the list, Parodi."

Berté began studying his files again. When he looked up, he found the Argentine tasked with looking after *Commendator* Olindo De Cillis standing in front of him.

"Sit, please," said Berté.

The man perched at the edge of his chair, looking at him uneasily. "Is there something wrong?"

Berté studied the man before him. He had eyes of an intense, almost periwinkle, blue. And in those blue eyes, there was much anxiety. So Berté sought to reassure him, "No, these are informal interviews. We're simply gathering background information.

"Signor Dalmasso, you are Argentine, correct? From where, specifically?"

"I'm from Parque Avellaneda, a neighborhood of Buenos Aires."

Berté once again lowered his eyes to the papers that he had in front of him. "I see that you've only been in Lungariva for a week."

"That's true, though I've been in Italy for ten years. In the past, I worked in La Spezia. When the man I was looking after died, my cousin Pedro asked me to come to Lungariva and help look after *Commendator* De Cillis. Pedro is having surgery so I'm filling in for him for a few weeks. But I can assure you the arrangement is perfectly legitimate and all my papers are in order."

Berté thought this was an odd thing to say but he let it pass, for the moment. "You speak Italian very well, almost without an accent."

"My family has roots in Veneto. And a lot of people spoke Italian in my neighborhood so I learned while growing up."

"Be more precise."

"Italian is a very common language in Argentina. My neighborhood was full of people whose parents or grandparents came from Italy, especially from the north. You see, after the first world war…"

Berté interrupted him. "I didn't mean about the history of Argentina, I meant about your family."

"Oh. Well, I don't know who my real parents are. I was adopted from an orphanage in Buenos Aires by a couple from Veneto. They had no other children. They came to Argentina after the war to look for work. At our house we spoke mostly Italian. I learned Spanish in school. So, ten years ago when they came back to Italy, I came with them. My Italian was already pretty good and, of course, after living here for ten years…"

"Do you know signora Van Der Meer?"

"I know *of* her. My employer, the *Commendatore*, talks about her all the time. I gather that she is kind to him and that he's rather in love with her. I do know he's very shocked by what's happened." This was accompanied by a little smile that Berté found strangely out of place.

"What about Licia Trevisan?"

"Isn't the countess named Licia?" asked Dalmasso, showing he was anything but inattentive.

"As it happens, yes. But we're interested in Licia Trevisan. Have you, or have you not, ever heard this name?"

"No… Never. I don't know anyone named Trevisan."

Berté sighed and dismissed him, watching thoughtfully as he walked away. That man was fifty years old, yet he looked younger than Berté did. Perhaps it was because he was skinny.

Or because you aren't.

He was adopted from an orphanage… What if he was her son, perhaps an unwanted son, born out of wedlock? He made some quick calculations. Van Der Meer was currently seventy-five years old, fifty years ago she was twenty-five. She was twenty-one when she arrived in Argentina, but how long did she stay there? He had to consult with Belli and check Van Der Meer's travel documents. They needed to find proof of when she left Argentina. On the other hand, the caregiver could have been the son or the brother of the real Trevisan. For some still unknown reason, he could have hated Van Der Meer to the point of looking for her, finally finding her, and taking his revenge.

He called Belli again. "Francesca… don't… I'm not…" Berté held the phone away from his ear and let Belli's frustration at his constant interruptions exhaust itself. "I'm not calling about that," said Berté when she paused for breath. "I need you to look into something else… Are you still there? OK. There was a hissing noise on the line for a moment. Anyway, I just finished questioning Dalmasso, De Cillis's caregiver. We need some background on him. You have his stats but it turns out he was an orphan who was adopted in Buenos Aires. See what you can find out about him and about the family that adopted him… Apart from what you already have in the file, all I know is that they were originally from Veneto and that they returned to Italy about ten years ago."

"Do you think he is the countess's son?"

"I don't know what to think anymore, Francesca, but let's try to look for more information." he said, ending the call. He'd never had a colleague as efficient and perceptive as Belli.

Or as patient.

For once, he had to admit, the Bastard was absolutely correct. And now, he needed a break. So far, it had been one of the worst days of his career. A coffee would be just the thing… with some of those little pastries…

As if he had read his thoughts, Parodi appeared and held the door open for a waiter carrying a tray. Berté gave him a grateful smile which soured slightly when he realized his coffee had arrived unaccompanied by so much as a dry cookie. What was that old saying about guests and fish?

L'ospite è come il pesce, dopo tre giorni puzza.

Yes. That was it. Berté sighed internally. And it had been three days. Even if he found Van Der Meer this afternoon, he still needed to get this case wrapped up, and soon.

His ringing phone interrupted his reverie. It was Sabatini.

"There have been some developments, Sir. They're transferring Brioschi to the hospital in Lavagna. It appears that he swallowed an entire bottle of sleeping pills. The paramedics found a new bottle completely empty at the foot of his bed along with an empty bottle of scotch."

"Did he leave a note?" Berté asked in a strangled voice.

"Nothing, Sir. The room was thoroughly searched. Nothing in writing and he didn't have a computer with him. I'm going to check his phone myself."

"Okay, Sabatini. Once Brioschi has been evaluated in Lavagna, have his doctor give me a call. And don't take no for an answer. Remind him it's a murder investigation if you have to."

Berté drank his coffee and placed a hand over his eyes. What a mess! If Brioschi survived and confessed to having killed out of jealousy before trying to commit suicide, what was he supposed to make of the Van Der Meer mystery? Was it all just an unlikely coincidence that had nothing to do with the case? Berté didn't believe in coincidences, especially unlikely ones. After spending an unpleasant half-hour on the phone with the chief of police he was again in need of a break. But before he could put his phone back into his pocket, it began ringing. It was Sabatini calling from the hospital. Berté felt slightly sick as he accepted the call. He didn't have a good feeling about this. Sabatini confirmed that Brioschi had arrived at the new hospital and then passed the phone to his new doctor. There was a moment of silence.

"Hello?"

"Hello, Doctor, I'm Deputy Assistant Chief of Police Berté."

"It's a pleasure. I'm Luca Filippi, the head of the intensive care department."

"I need to know about signor Brioschi. He's a key witness in an investigation I'm conducting."

"I'm afraid you can't talk to him and that you won't be able to for some time. He's still in critical condition. As you know, he swallowed a large dose of sleeping pills and drank a lot of alcohol.

We're doing everything we can but I can't promise you he'll ever regain consciousness or that he'll ever be able to answer your questions if he does."

"Please, ask Officer Sabatini to give you my direct number. I'd appreciate it if you'd keep me informed of even the slightest development. Day or night."

"Certainly. I'll let you know as soon as there is any change."

The call ended with a polite farewell.

This day had started badly and was getting worse by the minute. The threat to his career and his love life was bad enough. But now he had to feel guilty about an abusive loser like Brioschi! There really was no justice in the world.

That's the kind of thing we like to hear from a deputy assistant chief of police!

Normally, that would have gotten at least an ironic smile out of Berté but he was not in the mood. He would have liked to chuck it all and go sailing, but he had another Argentine to interview. Glancing at his files, he ordered Parodi to bring in Pablo Polledo, the polo player.

"Signor Polledo, good morning," began Berté, observing the young man who sat in front of him. "I'll only take a few minutes of your time."

Polledo was not very tall, but he had a muscular build and a handsome face. He had dirty-blonde hair, blue eyes and an open and confident look. Patty would have called him a "stud."

"So you're Argentine," Berté said, leafing through his files and noticing that Polledo was the same age as him. How depressing.

"Yes."

"And yet, you speak Italian very well." said Berté accusingly.

"Uhh, thank you. I try to speak without an accent, but it's difficult to control," said Polledo, shaking his head. "My fiancée, Rosalinda, gives me Italian lessons, but she's more attentive to my grammar..."

"You were born in..." Berté cut him short.

"In Pilar, the capital of polo. About sixty kilometers from Buenos Aires."

"Where do you live now?"

"For the past eight years, here in Italy. I'm a resident of Firenze. But I go back and forth. I play here in the summer and then return to Argentina in October and play there."

"So you're a professional player?"

"Yes. It's kind of a family tradition. My family was involved in polo and horse breeding before I was born."

"Why are you in Lungariva?"

"My girlfriend and I have some friends that have a house here… They invited us for a birthday party and we took the opportunity to take a small vacation, to change things up a bit. Is there something wrong?"

"No, no, on the contrary, Signor Polledo! It's just that what happened here forces me to ask everyone questions."

"A horrible event! Rosalinda is terrified. She wanted to leave right away, but it didn't seem right to me. Of course, we didn't know the people who… But we're very sorry."

The sad expression enhanced Polledo's cover-boy face. He was definitely charming. Most people would find him extremely likeable. But Berté didn't, not then. In the mood he was in, he would have picked a fight with the Pope.

"Where were you on the night of Easter?" he asked abruptly.

"In my room, with Rosalinda, as we told your colleague. We didn't see or hear anything. If we had, I would have certainly told you already!"

"And the following morning, you left the hotel to go on a jog…"

"As always. I have to stay in shape. I ride a horse, but I'm an athlete all the same! I left early that morning and ran for about fifteen kilometers. I didn't find out what had happened until I got back."

"You had a backpack with you, if I'm not mistaken."

"Yes. I usually carry one, especially at this time of year. I carry a sweatshirt, a light raincoat, and a bottle of water. If you want to check, come up to my room and have a look at it. But I don't understand what my sweatshirt has to do with anything."

"Just routine questions, Signor Polledo, don't worry. Now tell me about Argentina. Why did you leave your home country?"

"For love! I met Rosalinda in Buenos Aires and she convinced me to follow her back to Italy. I fell in love with Italy as well so I stayed. In Argentina I'm a decent player but there's a lot of competition. Here, I'm a champion!" Polledo smiled, showing his perfect white teeth.

Berté declined to observe that Rosalinda, according to the notes that Parodi had prepared, was very wealthy.

"You always lived in Pilar?"

"Yes. We had an *estancia* where my father bred horses. Splendid polo ponies. Our stable was famous."

"Honestly, I don't know much about it."

"My father sold horses to the best polo players in the world. However, when he died, we got out of the business."

"Ah, your father used to sell horses…"

"Yes, beautiful ones. But in the end, there were too many debts and I couldn't keep it going."

"Do you have brothers or sisters?"

"No, I'm an only child, and my mother is gone, too, now. My only family is Rosalinda, here in Italy."

"Do you know Signora Van Der Meer?"

"Not really. One evening we met at the reception desk and Rosalinda and I chatted with her for a few minutes. She's very kind, a true lady. She speaks excellent Spanish with an Argentine accent. Did you know she had been there many years ago?"

"Did she tell you anything about that? What city was she in? What did she do?"

"No… nothing. Only that she was there and that she knew Buenos Aires very well. If you ask her, I'm sure she'll tell you all about it. I don't think it's any sort of secret."

If only he could, thought Berté.

"Could you try to remember exactly what she told you about Argentina?"

Polledo looked at him, surprised. "She didn't say very much. It was just the sort of general conversation you might have with anyone. You know, 'Oh, you're from Argentina? I was there myself! I love Buenos Aires!' that kind of thing. Then we talked about me, and about polo. She said that she had been to polo matches herself and that her husband had played in his younger days. That's really all there was to it. We only talked for a couple of minutes."

"Did you also know Signor Sommariva and Signorina Ornella?"

"No. I never spoke to them. Again, we've only been here a few days, Rosalinda and I, and we spent most of our time out with our friends."

"I understand… The people who spend time at this hotel are a bit old for you two."

"Well, yes, but we like the Grand Hotel Miramare very much. It's a very traditional hotel, the service is excellent, and the food is outstanding."

"Very well, Signor Polledo. That's all for now. If you remember some other detail of your conversation with Signora Van Der Meer, please let us know. You are staying in Lungariva until…"

"We had planned to stay for a few more days, but this murder has really unsettled us. I don't know, we still haven't decided what to do…"

"I can imagine," observed Berté acidly. "On the other hand, as you didn't know the victims…"

"We didn't. I never spoke to them, I swear to you. But Rosalinda and I are sorry about the situation in general and for the countess in particular."

Morosely, Berté watched Polledo saunter away and out the door of the "Torture Chamber."

The three Argentines had not supplied him with much new information. He'd been so sure he was right.

To sum up, Polledo had left early in the morning with a backpack. The caregiver was an orphan with unknown parents. Gomez claimed he knew nothing of the countess, but he knew she was Italian, despite her foreign last name. Not a very impressive haul, he had to admit.

Only Berté and one other officer were still in the room. He'd had enough for the moment. It was time, he thought, to "interrogate" Frilli, the bartender.

The hotel bar was fairly crowded with guests busy getting in one more drink before dinner. Frilli was at his station behind the bar. As usual, he didn't look particularly pleased about anything. Service with a scowl.

Berté greeted him, "Good evening, Frilli." Frilli gave him a curt nod in response. "I'll take a martini." It was his favorite.

"You'll have to be patient, there's a lot of people." returned Frilli brusquely.

"No rush." Berté placed himself in front of the bartender and observed him thoughtfully while he worked. When a waiter appeared at the bar to pick up an order, Frilli said nothing, maintaining his sullen scowl. Berté found this odd. Bartenders were usually the life of the party, if only to make sure they raked in the tips.

"So you hate your job." Berté stated flatly, deciding to turn this into a genuine interrogation after all.

"Who told you that?" Frilli snapped, without looking up.

"You did. You're clearly unhappy."

"Well excuse me! Are you a cop or a psychologist?"

This wasn't starting well. Berté decided to change tack. "Actually, I'm the man who asks the questions – and gets answers."

Frilli only grunted. Berté felt a surge of annoyance. He had a choice. Either he dragged Frilli down to the police station and gave him the full treatment there – a tempting alternative – or he'd have to take it easy and just see what he could get out of him. Oh, what the hell. He had a dinner appointment and he could always have Parodi bring him in later if necessary. So nice and easy it was. "I heard that you were friends with Signor Sommariva," he said, making an effort to be friendly.

"*Friends* is a big word… He was just another customer."

Berté internally shook his head. Some people wouldn't do things the easy way if it beat them up in a dark alley. "Listen Frilli," said Berté conversationally, "I can see you're upset, and you're probably nervous talking to me because I'm a cop. So, since I'm such a friendly, easygoing guy, I'm going to give you a little advice: Answer my questions politely and truthfully. Because if you don't, I'm going to handcuff you and drag your sorry ass through the bar, out the lobby and down to the police station where someone will properly interrogate you. And, hey, it's late! Even police inspectors investigating murders go home at night so that would probably be sometime tomorrow. So how about it, Frilli? Would you like to leave work early tonight and take a ride in a police car? I'll even run the siren for you! Or would you like to stay here and answer my questions?"

The bartender froze and stared back at Berté with such a mixture of surprise, horror, and dismay that Berté had to bite his tongue to stop himself from laughing.

"I had nothing to do with the death of those two!" he finally managed to sputter. "It's… it's unfair. You've got no reason to investigate me!"

Berté bit his tongue harder. "That's for us to decide." he answered once he was sure he could do so with a straight face. "Now, answer my question and answer it fully and correctly. If you do not, we will find out and then you'll be facing a criminal charge even if you had nothing to do with the murder. Is that clear? Good. So tell me, how much money did you borrow from Sommariva?"

Frilli's face was ashen. "Nothing. I swear to you. I never borrowed anything from Sommariva. Yes, I admit, I've borrowed money from colleagues in the past. But never Sommariva. We did talk on occasion, but I didn't know him that well. Even if I had asked, he never would have lent me anything. It's the truth. I swear it."

Berté stared at him hard. "Is that your final word?"

"It is."

"In that case, I have another question."

Frilli now looked like he was about to be sick. "Where's my martini?"

Frilli poured one out of the shaker he had been clutching and staggered off.

Berté took a sip. It was excellent. 'A real asshole, but very good at his job.' Berté thought to himself.

A lot of people say exactly the same about you.

By now, it was almost 8:30. Grossi, the prosecutor, had arranged to meet him in a restaurant in the center of Lungariva called L'Insolita Zuppa. He'd heard about it, but he had never been there. He made his way to the lobby, where he came across Sabatini who was just on his way in.

"Sir, we went through Brioschi's room again but we didn't find anything interesting. Only a few more empty bottles. Gianasio and forensics turned the room upside down."

"Anything from his cell phone?"

"Nothing. In fact, he turned his phone off early yesterday evening."

Berté sighed. If only he had realized what bad shape Brioschi was in. But then again, what could he have done, really? The bartender had accused him of being a psychologist. But he wasn't. He was just a policeman who occasionally used psychological parlor tricks as part of his job. In that moment, he felt very tired. And he still had to face

Grossi.

"Listen, Sabatini, I have to have dinner with the prosecutor. But someone needs to be at the station in case we get some news about Van Der Meer. So don't stay here. Go back to the office."

"Fine. I'll go right now. Do you need a lift?"

"Do you know where L'Insolita Zuppa is?"

"Yes, Sir."

"Then let's go."

Five minutes later, Sabatini dropped him at the front door of the restaurant.

The place wasn't large. The colorful room radiated a sense of warmth. The restaurant had a playful feel, with eclectic decorations and lyrics from De Andrè's songs – the Genoese singer-songwriter beloved by all Ligurians – on the walls. Berté began humming "Un giudice," aka "A Judge," one of De Andrè's most famous hits. It seemed suitable, under the circumstances.

The prosecutor was sitting at a corner table, waiting for him. He was talking to a pretty young woman with a friendly smile, dressed like a chef. She even had the hat.

Berté walked up to the table and shook hands, both with the prosecutor and with the chef, who also turned out to be the owner. Grossi greeted him warmly. "It's good to see you, Deputy Assistant Chief Berté. How are you this evening?"

Oh, dear. It's even worse than I thought. You're a dead man.

Berté did not need the Bastard's prompting to realize that Grossi's excessive politeness was not a good sign. He was hanging by a thread here.

"Shall we order?" asked Grossi. "What do you suggest, Deputy Assistant Chief?"

The menu was short but tempting. Berté felt his stomach begin to rumble. It seemed like he had eaten that sandwich in a previous life. To make matters worse, he hadn't gotten any of those little pastries with his coffee. His martini hadn't even come with an olive!

Oh, the sacrifices you make in the pursuit of justice.

Berté chose an octopus and zucchini salad followed by cheese ravioli with a delicate tomato sauce, and freshly-caught, corn-crusted fish. Grossi largely agreed with Berté's choices but substituted red bucatini with fresh anchovies, toasted pine nuts, and lemon zest for the ravioli.

"To drink, does Greco di Tufo sound good, Deputy Assistant Chief?"

Berté died a little inside every time the prosecutor called him by his formal title but only nodded in response. And it *was* an excellent choice given the menu they had settled on.

"Now, while we wait, tell me how your day has gone. Any sign of Van Der Meer?" asked Grossi.

Berté didn't have much to report on the hunt for the countess. But he had quite a lot to report nonetheless. Brioschi's suicide attempt was a bombshell. Perhaps that would distract the prosecutor and get him off the hook, at least for the evening.

And it seemed to work. They'd been trying to puzzle out the significance of Brioschi's attempted suicide for at least two minutes before Grossi observed that it had been extremely careless of Berté to leave such an obviously desperate man alone and that Berté had managed to "lose" two possible suspects in a single day.

"It could've been him," Berté said, "but I ask myself how he would have managed to enter the hotel, steal the master key from the office, and slip away all without running into anyone. Even just trying to do all that would have required knowledge of the hotel that he couldn't have had. According to the doorman, Brioschi remained at the bar and didn't go up to the rooms at all."

"Let's hope he survives," said the prosecutor. "Otherwise, we're going to have a lot of unanswered questions. It wouldn't be the first time that a crime of passion was followed by remorse."

"According to the head of the ICU, the next few hours will be critical. One way or another, we'll probably know something tomorrow."

A waiter brought water, wine, and a bread basket. No focaccia. Berté sighed audibly. At least the wine was good. Berté took a healthy sip and then, throwing caution to the wind, launched into the topic of Van Der Meer's disappearance. "I confess I'm worried about Van de Meer. I wouldn't want the killer to…"

"You're not willing to let that go," the prosecutor interrupted him dryly, "but I don't think she is in any danger. More likely, she's made fools of us all." By which, of course, he meant Berté. Thankfully, he was interrupted by the arrival of the appetizers. For a few minutes they ate in appreciative semi-silence, interrupted only by remarks on the quality of the wine and the food. When the first course arrived, Berté brought up his conversation with the bartender and his claim that he had never borrowed money from Sommariva. He concluded his report by saying, "Gianasio was the one who interviewed him initially and she didn't think much of his truthfulness. She's inclined to believe the rumors she picked up from other staff members that he owed Sommariva money, which would give him a motive."

"But the coroner placed the time of death at around one in the morning," mused Grossi. "That would be a couple of hours after Frilli delivered the champagne."

"Exactly. So if it was the bartender, it means that he returned later to shoot Sommariva. But I'm not convinced that really holds together. Why kill Ferrari too?"

"Perhaps he didn't realize she was in the room. The shots do appear to have been a little wild. When he delivered the champagne, he wasn't allowed in the room and didn't know who else, if anyone, was present. But this is all speculation, isn't it? You know what my theory of the case is: Van Der Meer. Nonetheless, there's no reason to eliminate Frilli as a suspect. Keep digging, if you think it might lead somewhere. Have you turned up any more information on the countess and her history this afternoon?"

Berté briefly outlined what steps Belli was taking to uncover Van Der Meer's past as well as how she was digging into what had happened to the mysterious Licia Trevisan. But he said nothing about the recent interrogations with the Argentines. If his hunch came to nothing, he would look like a fool. And he'd done that enough for one day. He was just finishing up his report when Gianasio arrived at the restaurant.

Grossi greeted her warmly. "Excellent, Mariella, you've arrived just in time for dessert and coffee."

"Oh no! I've never eaten so many desserts and treats as I have during this investigation. Why just today, I ordered a coffee at the hotel and it came with this tray of little pastries! Just excellent! What's wrong, Berté?" exclaimed Gianasio.

"Oh, err, nothing. Just a touch of indigestion."

Soon, three servings of chocolate cake with coconut sauce and another three of panna cotta with fresh strawberries arrived at their table.

"How about you, Detective? Do you have anything new to report?" asked the prosecutor between bites.

Gianasio put down her spoon. "We thoroughly searched Brioschi's room. We found nothing of interest. It looks to me like a fairly run-of-the-mill suicide attempt. We know he was depressed and he already had access to the sleeping pills. He'd been taking them for some time. I found the prescription in his wallet. When it all got to be too much, he took them all at once and washed them down with a bottle of scotch. He was an alcoholic, so he had easy access to that, too. It could have been a spur of the moment decision."

"Any leads on Van Der Meer's whereabouts?"

"None so far. The bodyguard hasn't checked in with his agency all day. He hasn't contacted his family, either. Both his phone and Van Der Meer's are switched off so we can't trace them that way. The car hasn't been spotted either."

"Driving that car? Are you saying she's just vanished?"

"It wouldn't be that hard to disappear," interposed Berté. "All she would have to do is stay on less-traveled roads, make it to a private house and park the car in the garage. Once she's gotten rid of the car, she can move pretty freely, as long as she's careful. We both know how many fugitives there are in Italy. And Van Der Meer slipping through our net might be the best case scenario."

"Meaning what?" asked the prosecutor, annoyed.

"Meaning she may already be dead."

"Listen, Berté," said Grossi sternly. "If you think you know something, spit it out."

"Sir, let me be clear. I do have an idea. But, so far, I haven't got enough evidence to back it up. Until I have solid evidence, it's just a hunch. As you're the prosecutor in this case, I don't think it would be right to share a lot of half-formed speculations with you. *I* can follow up on hunches. But *you* are required to act only on evidence."

"He does like being mysterious," chimed in Gianasio. "But he is right more often than he's wrong."

"All I'm asking for, Sir, is a couple of more days to see if this idea pans out. If it doesn't, no harm done. And in the meantime, we can follow up on Van Der Meer, Brioschi, Frilli and all the rest."

Gianasio and Grossi exchanged a cryptic look. After a pause,

Grossi reluctantly nodded in agreement. Berté's phone rang, breaking the awkward silence. It was Belli. "Sir, we've finally got some information. I told you those nuns knew their business! The countess is actually one Lucia d'Andrea, born in Cordenons, just a few kilometers from where the real Licia Trevisan grew up. She was indeed a war orphan and ended up with Ursuline nuns in the province of Pordenone. We already knew she left for Argentina but the nuns had a record of the job she had waiting for her there."

"Which was?"

"She was going to be a maid in a private home. Now, I'm trying to see what information I can dig up on the family she was going to work for."

"That's excellent work, Belli, really excellent! I'm here having dinner with the prosecutor and your call could not have come at a better time. Well done!"

Berté hung up the phone and then relayed the message to Grossi and Gianasio.

"That's an excellent break in the case. If we could only find Van Der Meer, we might really have something. *Belli* has done some fine police work here. I think that calls for a toast, don't you? Waiter! Can we get some limoncello here?"

Well, at least this is ending on a positive note. And you still have a job! That's something.

An hour later found Berté navigating the stairs to his room. Thinking back, he realized that it had been an excellent meal. A slight dizziness due to the bottle of white wine and the limoncello made him light-headed enough to forget Grossi's sarcasm and the implied threats that had gone along with it. He made it to his room, turned on the light, and threw himself on the bed, still dressed. He wanted to sleep and forget the world for a few hours, but he was afraid that would be impossible. He now had 48 hours to prove his hunch and crack the case. If he didn't, Van Der Meer was going to get it in the neck. If, that is, they ever managed to find her. With a sigh he got up and went to the bathroom to wash his face. There was work to be done.

Why was he so convinced that Van Der Meer wasn't guilty? To be honest, he wasn't. In fact, he was convinced that the countess was guilty of something, but it wasn't these murders. Grossi had pressed him to explain his reasoning. One of the reasons he didn't was because he couldn't, not really. Can you explain a color? No. It's something you can see or you can't. He could *see* that Van Der Meer just didn't have the correct… psychology to have committed these murders even if Grossi couldn't. Oh, he was convinced that she was capable of killing if she needed to. But not like this, and not out of jealousy. Nonetheless, he was also convinced that she was hiding something, something in her past.

He settled himself at his desk to review the file. He didn't quite know what he was looking for, but he felt sure he'd know it when he saw it. The chair wasn't very comfortable but that was probably for the best. It might be an antidote for the limoncello and keep drowsiness at bay. He began to flip through the interview records, searching.

After two hours, he still had nothing. He had to laugh. An aging philanthropist with a secret identity is living in a grand hotel with her clandestine lover. The lover is murdered with a young woman in bed while the philanthropist absconds with her young bodyguard. You couldn't make this stuff up.

He returned to his work. He turned his attention to the binder of documents dealing with Van Der Meer's charity work that he had gotten from her ex-secretary in Varese Ligure. The elder Ferrari had been right. It was a pretty impressive testimony to her character. But after a while, the endless paeans of praise became even more boring than the pointless interviews of random hotel guests he had been studying before. Every document was either an official commendation from some organization or a heartfelt letter from somebody who had somehow personally benefitted from her generosity. All except one.

It was a letter written on the stationery of the Archdiocese of Genoa by a Monsignor Alberto Citterio thanking Van Der Meer for a contribution. But unlike the typical letter written by an organization, this one had something more. While the Monsignor was writing on behalf of the Archdiocese, there was something in this letter that hinted at a long history and at personal concern. Despite the letter's superficial formality, Berté was convinced that Van Der Meer and the Monsignor were old friends. And Van Der Meer could use an old friend just about now. What if she had gone to ground at his place?

He looked at his watch. It was almost two o'clock in the morning. Apart from the sound of the wind, there was complete silence. He couldn't call Belli at this time of the morning. But then again, he couldn't call Gianasio or Parodi either. Perhaps he could call the police station and see if anybody was either dedicated or foolish enough to still be in the office. He dialed the front desk and crossed his fingers. A sleepy desk officer told him that Belli was, in fact, still at work.

So Belli draws the short straw once again.

When the Bastard was right, the Bastard was right. He solemnly swore to himself that he would get her a promotion when this case was closed. She'd earned it several times over.

"Listen, Francesca," he said to her as soon as she answered, "I need a favor. Look into a Monsignor Alberto Citterio. He works or worked for the Archdiocese of Genoa. In particular, I need to know where he lives."

"Right away, Sir. That shouldn't be too difficult. Certainly easier than tracking down families who lived in Argentina in the 1950s! I'll call you as soon as I know anything."

As he waited, it occurred to Berté that he might as well do something useful. It wasn't as though he were going to sleep while he waited for Belli's call. A lazy writer is no writer at all, he thought to himself as he opened the "short stories" folder on his laptop.

*****

An hour passed. Berté was so engrossed in his work that when his phone finally rang, he half-jumped out of his chair, his heart hammering. It was Belli.

"Sir, I've got the information you asked for. I'll email you the details. But it turns out that the Monsignor is originally from Arenzano and he lives there now, with his sister. That's just the other side of Genoa, only about thirty kilometers from here."

'Jackpot!' thought Berté, pumping his fist over his head and glad that no one could see him. "Send me everything you've come up with. And thank you. You're amazing. There's one more thing…"

"Yes, Sir?"

"Go to bed!"

"Yes, Sir," Belli chuckled. "Goodnight."

Berté stretched and headed for the bathroom, humming under his breath. He reluctantly concluded that he couldn't really barge into a respected priest's house at three o'clock in the morning just because he had written a nice letter to someone. Dinner had been excellent. He'd gotten some decent writing done. He'd even gotten to twist Brioschi's tail. And now he had a lead to follow. The day hadn't turned out so badly after all.

The Fourth Day

Looking at himself in the mirror was not the ideal way to start the day, especially this morning. The only thing that could be said for all the stubble was that it covered quite a lot of his face. What could be seen was an unattractive greenish-yellow that said a lot about both the quality of the limoncello and the state of his liver. He had dark purple circles under his eyes and, adding insult to injury, a pimple peeking out of the bristles on his chin.

One of the few blessings of his teenage years was that he had never suffered from acne. It seemed somehow indecent to start now. Eyeing himself critically, he decided he needed a good shave and a hot shower. Perhaps it would also wake him up. He hadn't slept a wink all night and he had a lot to do today. Starting with finding Van Der Meer a.k.a. Licia Trevisan, a.k.a. Lucia d'Andrea. The thought filled him with adrenaline. She had a lot of questions to answer.

The state of his relationship with Marzia had also contributed to his insomnia. He couldn't go on sleeping – or, rather, not sleeping – under the same roof, one flight of stairs away from her, indefinitely. He had decided to wait until he closed the case before he sorted out his personal life. But that could take months – or maybe forever – unless he got a break soon.

Once he had finished his ablutions, he eyed his reflection critically. He looked almost human now.

I wouldn't be so sure. The mirror is awfully foggy.

He was meeting a monsignor – and hopefully a countess – today, so he ought to dress respectfully. His blue jacket and white shirt were perfect. But with jeans, though. There was no sense in overdoing it. He sat on the armchair in front of the window from which he could see an ancient olive tree. It wasn't beautiful, but it had character and he had grown rather fond of it. He had promised himself that he would wait until a decent hour before beginning the hunt. He checked his phone. It was just after seven thirty in the morning. Time to go!

He got up, picked up his coat and holstered his Beretta 92. He probably wouldn't need it. But he wasn't taking any backup with him, so better safe... Dinner had been hours ago and Berté was hungry. He also needed coffee... badly. Giustina brought him a double shot of espresso, and Berté followed it up with two large portions of an apple and pine nut cake, a thick slice of bread spread with Nutella, and to finish, a dozen fragrant homemade *canestrelli*, traditional Ligurian shortbread cookies with a hint of lemon and shaped like a flower with eight petals.

He tried to savor the moment, knowing full well that this might be his only peaceful interlude of the day. He paused to scan a copy of *Il Secolo XIX* just to see if there were any more incriminating photos featuring him and Gianasio. Finally, he smiled absent-mindedly at Marzia's calycanthus flowers and left the dining room.

On the counter in the reception area, next to an Easter egg decorated with ducks and chicks, sat both of Marzia's enormous cats. Their front paws were crossed as if in disdain, and they stared at him accusingly, their yellow eyes unblinking.

As if the Bastard wasn't enough, now he was getting dissed by cats. Alright. Fine. Yes, he had been kind of ignoring her. He hadn't even responded to her brief message. But it was difficult! He pleaded mentally with the unforgiving felines.

Giving in, he retraced his steps and rang the reception bell.

"I'll be right there," trilled Marzia's voice.

Berté waited nervously. He wasn't sure what he would say. He didn't need the Bastard to tell him that, under the circumstances, it would probably be something stupid.

As she made her way out of the office, Berté eyed her critically. She looked good, very good. Certainly much better than he did that morning, despite his efforts.

She greeted him warmly. "I didn't expect to see you," she said, giving him a hug.

"Sorry if I've been M.I.A.," muttered Berté, reluctantly breaking away from her.

"I'm not surprised. You've got a lot on your mind. And you've got more important things to do."

"It's not like that! It's just..."

"I know it's not like that." laughed Marzia. "But this case is important and the clock is ticking. And I'm not going anywhere.

Marco will be gone for months. We've got plenty of time."

"I feel like a fool…"

She stopped him with a light kiss. "You're not. Now get out of here and go catch a murderer."

Berté knew good advice when he heard it, at least this time, and made his way out of the pensione without another word. He got into his car and headed north. Once he made it to the highway and through the toll booth, he called Parodi. "Where are you?" he asked the instant he picked up.

"I'm at the station. But I was just about to call you to see if you wanted to go to the hospital with me to see if Brioschi is able to talk. Shall I pick you up?"

"No, I'm going to Arenzano, and don't ask me why, I'll explain it to you later. But don't worry about going to the hospital. Text me Dr. Filippi's number. I'll call him now and see how Brioschi is doing. Any other news?"

"No news on the hunt for the countess. There are no credit card charges and no phone calls."

"Well, watch out for the press, Costa in particular. We're trying to keep a lid on this."

"Alright, Sir. Ah, Gianasio wants to talk with you. She tried your cell phone but it went to voice mail so she called the Grand Hotel to see if you were there."

"Okay. I'll call her. How is the dumpster search going?"

"Two officers are working on it. They're also checking the charity bins where people drop off used clothes for Caritas."

"It's a long shot, but we need to cover all the bases. Let's make sure we do a thorough sweep."

"Yes, Sir."

"And make sure you keep a close watch on those three Argentines. If they disappear as well, we might as well join them."

"Sabatini has officers assigned to watch them and log their movements. If you want to know, I can tell you what they had for breakfast and when they went to the bathroom. They aren't going anywhere."

"See that they don't!"

"Yes, Sir. When are you coming back?"

"Soon. Bye, Pasquale." As he ended the call, a smile lit his face. He took a sadistic pleasure in calling Parodi by his first name. He knew how much it annoyed him and he also knew that Parodi had far too much respect for Berté's position to complain about it.

And you think I'm an obnoxious jerk.

Berté had to admit there was something in what the Bastard said. He could not resist teasing Parodi but he knew that Parodi was his finest and most reliable colleague – and that included the human wonder Belli. He had once described him as "God's policeman." Parodi was as honest and forthright as it was possible to be. There weren't many like him in the police force – or anywhere, really – but especially in the police, where self-serving bureaucrats, crooks, and back-stabbing bastards were too often the norm. No, he didn't miss Milan at all.

Parodi's text message with the doctor's number derailed this unpleasant train of thought. Grateful for the distraction, Berté dialed the number.

"This is Deputy Assistant Chief Berté. Is this Dr. Filippi?"

"Yes indeed. Good morning! I assume you're calling for an update on Signor Brioschi?"

"That's correct. How is he doing?"

"The good news is that he's stable. The bad news is that will be quite some time before he's out of danger. To be honest, he might not make it. So you're going to have to wait."

"He's not able to talk?"

"Absolutely not. He's not even conscious yet."

"Thank you, Doctor. Please contact me if anything changes."

"Certainly. I'll be in touch."

It was a crystal clear day and in between the tunnels on the highway, the dark green of the Tyrrhenian Sea stretched out before him. There was little traffic, and in less than half an hour he had passed Genoa. Berté didn't normally make it a habit of dropping in on senior clerics without an appointment but this was a special case. He wasn't absolutely certain Van Der Meer was there but Arenzano wasn't that far and, if he had guessed wrong, he could always ask Monsignor Citterio about her past. He might even learn something useful.

The phone rang. He was about to cancel the call – he wanted to plan his encounter with Citterio – when he saw it was Gianasio.

Better take that one.

"Berté, where are you?"

"Near Arenzano. Don't ask. I'll explain later. If it works out."

"Damn it, Berté, you're freelancing again! If you are out interviewing another witness, I had better hear about it before Grossi does. Because if you let me make a fool of myself again, there's going to be another murder to investigate. I have…" His reception was mercifully interrupted by a short tunnel.

When the connection was restored, Berté quickly moved on to another topic. "Parodi said you have been trying to reach me since before breakfast. What's up?"

"Yeah. I've got some interesting news about Sommariva's son, Paolo. He was the guy who had supposedly disappeared in India."

"Tell me."

"He's here."

"Where? In Italy?"

"At the hotel. I just spoke with him. He admitted to calling his father shortly before he was murdered. He claims that Sommariva was initially quite hostile toward him because he feared he was going to ask him for money. He also told him about the loan he made to the bartender."

"Oh really? So he was lying!"

"It certainly seems that way. According to Paolo Sommariva, his father even told Van Der Meer about the loan and she advised him to be patient because she felt sorry for Frilli."

"She certainly never told me that."

"Would you have expected her to? A proper lady doesn't discuss other people's debts." opined Gianasio.

"Whatever. But she's going to discuss them now. I'll add that to the list of questions we're going to ask once we find her. And you may have been right all along about Frilli. That improves the odds on him quite a bit."

"He's certainly the only person we've identified so far that really benefits from the murders. As far as we can tell, there's no written record of this loan so by eliminating Sommariva, Frilli eliminated the debt. Ferrari was just in the wrong place at the wrong time."

"That is logical, I have to admit. Let's keep Frilli under surveillance, too. If he's guilty, he's got to be under a lot of pressure to disappear." ordered Berté.

"And I don't know if it really has any bearing on the investigation, but in the end Paolo Sommariva left things right with his father. He even promised him he would come to see him in Lungariva."

"It would have been a nice family reunion, but he left it a bit late. Where was this Paolo before he turned up at the hotel?"

"In Rome!" laughed Gianasio. "I guess he just doesn't like his sister because, regardless of what he told her, he never 'disappeared' in India at all, though he does go back and forth between Italy and India for work. And that's not the only thing she got wrong! He's also married and has two children. And he might have dabbled in Eastern philosophy in the past but now he's more Catholic than the Pope. He even insists on attending Mass in Latin! In fact, that's why he's only just turning up now. He had been granted an audience with His Holiness but it was set up months in advance. He'd be damned if he was going to miss that!" said Gianasio, unable to resist snickering at her own joke. "Anyway, he read about his father's death in the paper so he turned up here as soon as he could... after he'd had his audience, that is."

"Am I wrong or is this guy a bit off? I mean, his father's murder is front-page news and he's off to meet the Pope?"

"At least a bit. But his, ahh, devotion to religion does give him an excellent alibi. He spent the night of Easter at a prayer vigil with dozens of people. I'm going to check, of course, but I'm pretty sure they will all testify he was there in Rome on the night of the murder."

"Hmph. That doesn't necessarily clear him. He could have arranged the murder with an accomplice. Having prayer vigils and popes to alibi you is almost too good to have happened accidentally."

"You could be right." agreed Gianasio. "When will you be back?"

"Soon, very soon."

"You *are* a lone wolf, Berté." Gianasio sounded annoyed again.

"Look. I'm sorry. I swear you'll be the first person I tell, as soon as I have something to tell, that is."

"Yay." said Gianasio with an unequivocal hint of sarcasm. "To think that you'd actually tell your partner what's going on. That I should be so honored!"

"Alright, alright. Point taken. I'll see you soon." Berté hung up and exited the highway. He had arrived.

The villa was part of a well-landscaped residential complex. It smelled like money. Berté rang the bell, badge in hand. Within seconds, the door was opened by a maid, complete with uniform. She seemed startled at the sight of him. Maybe it was the ponytail.

"Deputy Assistant Chief Berté." he said, waiving his badge. "I need to speak with Monsignor Citterio."

"I'm sorry… The Monsignor is resting and said he wasn't to be disturbed so…" responded the maid, torn between church and state.

"Who is it, Teresa?" asked a worried voice from somewhere inside the house. "It's the police, ma'am." responded Teresa.

"The police? I'll be right there!" A very elderly woman soon appeared in the hallway and Teresa gratefully retreated. Berté, badge still in hand, explained once again that he needed to speak to the monsignor."

"Certainly. Please come in. I'll go and let my brother know you are here. Is he expecting you?"

Berté wanted to say that he should have been but simply shook his head.

The house was decorated in rather old-fashioned style, with dark and massive furniture. He waited in a living room where, in addition to Chesterfield sofas and armchairs, there was a large mahogany bookcase in which the numerous volumes were neatly arranged and without a speck of dust. This Teresa apparently knew her business. Berté had a look at the titles. Almost all of them were essays on theology and philosophy. He picked one up at random. It was by Jean Leclercq and entitled *Jean de Paris et l'ecclésiologie du XIIIe siècle*. This was heavy stuff.

"Good morning, Inspector, I see you are interested in ecclesiastical history."

Berté turned to find himself facing the monsignor. He was more or less what he expected. Citterio was thin, wearing a cassock and had short, thinning gray hair. One thing he had not necessarily expected was that the monsignor was sporting a friendly smile that immediately put him at ease.

"Unfortunately, I don't think my French is up to it," answered

Berté, showing him the book. Berté did not speak a word of French.

"A pity! It's a great read!" exclaimed the monsignor, "And Jean de Paris was a great thinker, though underappreciated among political philosophers. Do you recall the dispute between the king of France, Philip the Fair, and Pope Boniface VIII?"

"Not personally."

Monsignor Citterio laughed heartily.

"Well, it might have happened in the 13th century but it's a timeless story about the competition for power. We can't know the past entirely, but the insights you do get from the study of history tell you a great deal about the future. The characters change, but the plots remain the same."

"Without a doubt the study of the past is fundamental to understanding men," Berté agreed, returning the book to its place. "I suppose, in a sense, I'm a historian too, though my studies are not on quite that grand a scale. And as you say, the characters change, but the plots remain the same."

"You're right. There is very little new under the sun. But I don't think that you came here for literary advice," said the priest sitting on the sofa. "Please, take a seat."

"I did not, Monsignor," affirmed Berté, sitting next to him. "I apologize for my abruptness but time is pressing so I will get right to the point. I am here because I believe you know where I can find Signora Van Der Meer."

"Indeed I do, Inspector. In fact, I have been looking forward to meeting you." said the monsignor, smiling grimly.

"You have?" asked Berté, stunned.

"Oh, yes. In fact, if you hadn't already turned up at my door, I was going to give you a call and invite you for a visit. Out of curiosity, how did you connect her with me? Licia told me she had a good impression of you, but I admit I am surprised."

"So where is she?"

"In a moment. First, there's a condition."

Berté raised his right hand to interrupt him.

"Don't concern yourself," continued the prelate overriding Berté's silent objection, "I would never ask you to do anything unethical. In any case, Licia hasn't killed anybody."

"Monsignor, my work has rules, just like yours, so I must be the judge of what is ethical and what isn't. And as much as I admire your faith in her, the assurances of a friend, even a godly one, aren't evidence."

"Very well. Let me finish and then you can draw your own conclusions. Licia is in a very difficult situation. You are asking her to place her life in your hands and she wants assurances that you can be trusted. Her life really is at stake."

"I'd surmised as much." Berté replied gravely.

"And you have not yet answered my question. How did you trace her back to me?"

"I read a letter you wrote to Signora Van Der Meer thanking her for some charitable donation or other. It didn't ring true to me. Or rather, it rang altogether too true. There was something more there than there should have been. After that, I just followed my intuition. And it led me here."

"We've known each other for many years now. She's an admirable person and not just because she has been such a great friend to the needy. You can't imagine how many unfortunate people she has helped with her generosity. I owed her sanctuary and counsel. She had already decided to contact you for help before you arrived. I was about to call you, but that's not necessary now. You tracked her down on your own. Well done."

"It's only my job, Monsignor. And you are stalling. Where is she?"

"I'm getting to that. She's willing to meet you, here, at my house, to tell you her story. But her life is in danger. Before she makes herself a target, I want your assurance that you will do everything possible to protect her."

"Protecting human life is a policeman's primary duty."

"You're going to have to do a little better than that, Inspector. She needs physical protection around-the-clock. I want you to swear that you will assign an armed officer to her until this matter is settled. I'm confident that you'd do that anyway once you hear her story, but I want your personal promise nonetheless."

An image of the Grand Hotel swarming with officers flashed through Berté's mind. "I can promise you that she will be protected. But whether that's in a hotel room or a jail cell I can't say until I take her statement and understand who she is running from and why."

"I'm not asking you for immunity, just protection. She knows what she has done and she knows what she is going to face."

"Very well, Monsignor. Call her in."

"Yes, Inspector, you're right. She is here. I'll go and get her. Then I'll leave you two alone. You have a lot to discuss."

When Van Der Meer finally made her appearance, she might have been stepping on the stage at La Scala. She had the bearing of a great actress and when she sat down across from Berté, she seemed to fill the room.

Not the best witnesses, actresses. Let's hope this one can tell truth from fiction.

"You have to believe me, Inspector," she began.

Berté let out a sigh. "No, I don't. You are a fugitive, Signora, so I am obliged to treat everything you say with caution. Nonetheless, if you tell me the truth – all of it! – then I will believe you. But I warn you, if you lie to me, your position will not protect you. Why did you leave the Grand Hotel Miramare yesterday, Signora Lucia d'Andrea?"

Berté was disappointed. He'd been looking forward to dropping this bombshell for two days but the bomb didn't go off. The countess only smiled, sadly. "Well done, Inspector. I've been trying to keep my secrets for more than fifty years and you discover them all in two days. What else do you already know?"

"Don't you worry about what I know. Tell me what you know."

"Very well. You're right. I should start by saying that it was fear, not guilt, that brought me to Monsignor Citterio. He has been my confidante for a long time and I respect him deeply. After consulting with him, we both agreed that I should speak with you."

Berté simply observed her, saying nothing. The lady had class, he had to admit. And she was tough, betraying no emotion beyond a certain sadness. Having fled from her hotel with just the clothes on her back, she still exuded elegance, despite her slightly disheveled thick blond hair and the dark circles under her eyes.

"My bodyguard helped me escape from the Grand Hotel and I had him drive me here. He agreed…"

"Signora," Berté interrupted, "You know I'm not interested in your travel arrangements. Start talking."

"I can see you are impatient, Inspector, but my story is not a simple one to tell."

"Why don't you start at the end. Who were you fleeing from

yesterday when you left the hotel?"

"That would mean nothing to you. No, with your permission, I prefer to tell you everything from the beginning. Or, at least, from the moment when, on a beautiful day in May 1957, a twenty-one-year-old young woman from Friuli named Lucia d'Andrea, an orphan with no friends, boarded the *Augustus* bound for Argentina in search of a new life."

Berté took out the photo he had "borrowed" from Gianna Ferrari and handed it to her. Signora Van Der Meer, or Signorina Trevisan, or D'Andrea – he no longer knew what to call her – took the old, yellowed photo in her hands and studied it with regret. She didn't ask how he got his hands on it, and he was grateful for that. "We were so young! And naive… and happy." she murmured. "I remember the exact moment when one of the men we were traveling with took this picture of us. He was from Friuli, like us, and like us he had left Italy behind and was seeking his fortune out in the world. He asked for Licia's address and kept his word by sending us the photograph. I wonder what ever happened to him? There were many like him, on that ship."

"Did you and Licia Trevisan know each other before the trip?"

"No. I came from Cordenons, she came from Maniago. Our two villages are not far from one another, but we had never seen each other before. Licia and I met in Genoa, right before the *Augustus* departed. We were both on our own, and at that age you make friends easily. We shared our hopes and our dreams, as young women do. As children, we had both experienced war. Both of us were orphans and without any family. I had studied with the nuns, while Licia had worked as a maid for a family in Pordenone until she decided to try her luck and join her fiancée, who had left the year before for Buenos Aires. Fiancé…" she laughed grimly. "It sounded like such an important word to me back then. She was under the illusion that he was expecting her and that he was setting up their love nest. She had worked two jobs to scrape together the money for her ticket."

"Wasn't he expecting her?"

"Oh, yes. That bastard knew she was coming! But there was no 'love nest' waiting for her." Van Der Meer's face reddened with indignation.

"Please, continue."

"I still remember it as if it were yesterday. That white ocean liner was already a new world to us, with its mysteries, its passengers overflowing with dreams… And Buenos Aires! Ah, Buenos Aires was a *city*… vibrant, alive… and free of the war. It was like nothing I'd ever seen with its amazing palaces and its *Avenidas*. I knew then that I loved to travel and wanted to explore the entire world." Van Der Meer smiled sadly, stroking her friend's face on the photograph.

"Licia and I parted ways at the port," she continued. "The nuns had arranged a position for me. I was supposed to work as a governess for a family. When we parted, Licia cried as she bid me farewell. She asked me to visit her at the address that Mario, her fiancé, sent her. I have never forgotten that address… *El Marabú, calle Maipú 359*. Licia had repeated that address to me so often during the trip that it is still imprinted in my memory." Van Der Meer looked down and held her face in her hands, tears streaming.

Berté said nothing. There was a time to push a witness and this was not the time. When she had regained her composure, she said, "Getting used to a new way of life was not easy, nor romantic. My new job didn't last long. My employer and his brother both lived in the house and they were beasts, animals. I will spare you the sordid details but it wasn't long before I fled and I still feel guilty today about leaving those children in the care of those two brutal pigs.

"Where did you go?"

"Where do you think? I was a young girl in a big city with only one friend. So I went there, to Licia's. But it was almost as bad. What I found was not a love nest for her and Mario. Instead it was a sleazy dance hall, crowded with businessmen and land owners who were all there to do what they couldn't do in polite society. The place was full of gambling, prostitution, and worse."

Berté said nothing but his disgust must have shown on his face.

"You think I am a hypocrite. That I'm hiding my disgraceful past behind a façade of high standards and morality." she commented bitterly.

"I don't judge you at all, Signora," Berté interrupted.

"That's not true, you do. You are. I could tell you were judging me when we first met, before you knew any of this."

"Evaluating people is part of my job," Berté said, trying to soften his tone.

"Oh, but you're right. You are right to judge me. Not all the girls who emigrated to Argentina became dancers, *entraineuses* or *coperas*, those girls who were paid based on the number of drinks they were able to get men in bars to buy for them. But Licia and I, left with no family and no friends… we had little choice. It was either that or become piece-working slaves in some sweatshop. Perhaps we should have done that, a lot of girls in the Italian community in Buenos Aires did. But in our pride and ambition, we thought we deserved better. We pay for everything, Inspector, especially for our ambition."

"Again, I make no moral judgment. That's between you and God. But it is my job to ask questions. What happened to Licia Trevisan?" Berté pressed her.

"What didn't happen to Licia? It's not a pretty story and it would take me hours to tell you all the details. It isn't something I talk about. In fact, including you, I've only told three people about those years in Buenos Aires."

"Who are the other two?"

"Monsignor Citterio, whom you've just met, and my husband, Count Van Der Meer. A man without prejudice who accepted me for who I was, even after hearing the story of my past. He was the love of my life."

"And what about signor Sommariva?"

"Roberto was, I'm embarrassed to admit, a fling. He was an effort at recapturing what I had lost. But he wasn't Victor. I was a fool. And now, I am distraught thinking that he died because of me. If I tell you my story it is only because I'm convinced that you will see justice done and make sure his murderer pays."

Berté inclined his head in acceptance.

"Licia and I tried to limit ourselves to being *coperas* but it was a slippery slope," continued Van Der Meer, "and Licia suffered quite a bit of abuse from her beloved Mario. He was responsible for recruiting naive girls like us, and he demanded more and more of her. I limited myself to encouraging customers to drink. I never took it further. What saved me was the education I received in boarding school. After a while, I wrangled a job working in the office and helping with the books. It didn't pay much, but it kept me off the floor of the club and out of harm's way. And a good thing, too. Because one evening, Frondizi's dog, Luis Margaride, ordered a raid on the nightclub. He became much more famous years later. But even then, he was a bastard and he had been given the job of restoring 'morality' with a truncheon and a gun. No nightclub was safe, and since gambling and prostitution really were going on at *El Marabú*... Margaride's men were famous for their brutality. They enjoyed beating and torturing people... and worse.

"Did that happen to Licia?"

Van Der Meer lowered her head sadly. "It was a terrible night," she continued. "I've never forgotten. The policemen broke into the club and began to beat people, men, women, employees, customers, everyone except those rich enough to bribe them or powerful enough to frighten them. And it wasn't just beatings. I could hear gunshots as well."

"What did you do?"

"What could I do? I hid and prayed that they wouldn't find me. After a while, everything went quiet. When I thought it might be safe again, I crept out and started looking for Licia. But apart from the wrecked furniture and the bloodstains, the club was completely empty. I searched the basement and the rooms above the clubs, but nothing. Eventually, I left *El Marabú* and returned to the little room we shared. Where else was I going to go? The next day, I walked by the club but it was being guarded by the police and they were removing all the records from the office. That was even worse because a lot of those records had my name on them."

Van Der Meer stopped for a moment, shaking, her eyes far away. After all these years, the terror had not left her. "I waited for Licia for a week. But the rent was due and I knew they were hunting for me. I couldn't stay and I couldn't go. So I disappeared. I took what money the two of us had and fled. I feel guilty about that to this day. When I could, I tried to track Licia down. But there was no trace of her. She was nothing to them. Just a girl in a bar. I can only imagine that she was killed during the raid and that the police dumped her body somewhere. I'm sure that saved them a lot of paperwork." said Van Der Meer bitterly, suppressing a sob.

"But 'Licia' didn't really disappear, did she?"

Van Der Meer hung her head. "No, Inspector, she did not. I didn't think the police would be looking for Licia, since she was either dead or in jail. So I took her identity documents and became Licia Trevisan. It wasn't that hard to do, back then. We looked very similar anyway, and in a grainy, black and white photo…"

"And when you disappeared, what did you do? Where did you go?"

"There was one regular at the club, Marcelo, who I had gotten to know. Most of the other patrons were awful. But Marcelo was different, a gentleman. I even saw him outside of the club a few times when he was in town. He had an estancia – La Maruca, in the Pampas – so I hopped on a bus and went out to find him. I wasn't sure what I was going to do, but I needed somewhere safe to stay and I thought perhaps he could help me get back to Italy or at least out of the country."

"But it didn't turn out that way, did it?"

Van Der Meer smiled, in spite of herself. "Marcelo was a good man but for some things, he was useless. His wife had died several years earlier and she had been the one who actually ran the business side of the estate. That wasn't something an Argentine man could admit, back then, or even now, I imagine. When I turned up, Marcelo took me in and was kind to me. He knew I had been doing the books at El Marabú so he asked me to have a look at his. What a mess! The estate was near bankruptcy and Marcelo had no idea. It took many months – years, really – to straighten things out and get the estate back on its feet. So no, I didn't go back to Italy."

"So instead of returning to Italy, you and Marcelo got married."

"No. We did not. We might have done, but his son made that impossible. He was ten years old when I first met him and he came to resent me bitterly, especially after I more-or-less became the Doña of the estancia."

"Well, it can take some time for children to… "

Van Der Meer cut him off. "No. You don't understand. It was much more than that. This child didn't just resent me, he hated me. There was something wrong with him. He didn't sulk. He had violent outbursts. And not just screaming or throwing things. He *killed* things when he was angry. I don't mind admitting that I was terrified of him, even at the age of ten. It got so bad that his father eventually sent him off to boarding school. When he was gone, life was good, a bit boring perhaps, but good. Apart from the cattle that were the estancia's main business, Marcelo raised polo ponies. He loved the game and it was great fun to watch, though I never played. But his son came home for school vacations, and every time he did, it was worse."

"When you say he killed things…" asked Berté with forced casualness.

"It wasn't just flies, if that's what you're asking. There were small animals like mice, occasionally animals he had taken from the farmyard. There was a puppy, once. He left that one in my room."

"So how did all this end?" asked Berté, disquieted despite himself. He had a bad feeling about where this was going and he much preferred a nice, healthy crime of passion.

Van Der Meer smiled sardonically. "If you want me to cut to the chase, Marcelo died suddenly and I ran off with all the money. Oh, wipe that look off your face. I did not kill Marcelo. I suppose you could say that Marcelo killed himself. He had always been a drinker and the problems with his son only made it worse. He had had such hopes for him! But eventually, even Marcelo had to admit that his son wasn't just going through a phase and that there was something very, very wrong. One day, when he was sixteen, he came home for the Christmas holiday and he, he, tried to kill me. He had his hands around my throat and I couldn't scream, but I was doing my best to fight back and Marcelo heard the sounds of the struggle. He struck his son from behind and then the two of them fought until they were physically separated by two of the ranch hands. It was terrible. I will never forget it."

"So what happened?"

Van Der Meer shrugged. "What could happen? He had tried to kill his father. He was thrown out of the house and told never to come back. But even then, Marcelo couldn't bring himself to completely disown him and kept paying his school fees. After that, Marcelo took to drinking, and he drank *a lot*. Cirrhosis eventually killed him."

"And how is it that you ran off with the money?" Berté prompted.

"Marcelo and I had been together for six years. He knew he was dying and he felt guilty, guilty about what his son had become and guilty about what would happen to me once he was gone. Even disgraced, his son was going to be his legal heir and he knew that I couldn't stay in Argentina. The police might not be looking for me anymore, but his son would and I would end up like that puppy. So he liquidated what assets he could and transferred them to me. When the time came, I would be wealthy and free. His son would inherit the estancia and, while there wouldn't be much cash to go with it, the estate was in far better shape than it was when I had arrived six years before. Marcelo had his faults, but he was a good man, and he did his best to make things right, both for me and for his son."

"And when Marcelo died?"

"We both knew it was coming, and I made what plans I could. I stayed with him to the end, but I didn't stay for the funeral. I was on an airplane the day after he died. His son had already tried to kill me once and when he realized that most of Marcelo's cash and investments were gone…"

"Didn't Marcelo leave his son anything in writing explaining what he had done?"

"He did. He also left me a final letter which I still have. It's very personal. If you insist, I can show it to you. But we both knew that it wouldn't matter. Marcelo's son would never accept what his father had done. And he was violent, paranoid, and dangerous. There would be no reasoning with him and I did not intend to try. I was on the verge of starting a new, exciting life and I wasn't going to have that life cut short because I observed the finer points of etiquette and offered a son condolences for his father's death. I am not a fan of irony."

"And when you left, you used Licia Trevisan's documents."

"Yes, of course. Marcelo knew my real name, Lucia d'Andrea, and, of course, his son knew me by the same name. So when I left the country, I traveled on Licia's passport so he couldn't track me down. You may find it hard to believe now, but I knew what Marcelo's son would do if he found me and I was in genuine fear for my life."

"Just as you were yesterday." interjected Berté.

"Yes, I was." Van Der Meer eyed him thoughtfully. "But I will come to that. When I took up my new life, I abandoned the name Lucia d'Andrea and I became Licia Trevisan. As I said, it wasn't that hard. I remember I was a little nervous the first time I renewed 'my' passport, but after that, I was home free. When I left Argentina, I traveled. First, I went to the United States. I loved New York and Los Angeles. You have to remember, it was the late sixties and I was young, wealthy, and beautiful." Van Der Meer blushed slightly, the first time Berté had ever seen her betray any sort of embarrassment. "And I was not the pillar of rectitude I pretend to be now. While I can't say I'm proud of the way I behaved, I also can't deny that I had a lot of fun. Those were wild years, but exhausting. After a few years in the States, I needed a rest and decided to take a long cruise. I was hooked. Traveling first class on a cruise ship was nothing like traveling on the *Augustus*. So I sailed and saw the world for a few years. That changed me. I'll never forget my first trip to India and what I saw there. Poverty is a funny thing. It's easy to ignore until you really *see* it. And then you see it everywhere. I realized that I had an opportunity to make a difference so, in a small way, I became a philanthropist, a passion that Victor and I shared."

"Ah, count Van Der Meer. And how did you meet him?"

"At an embassy party in South Africa. Victor had been a widower for a few years and Christine, his daughter, was still a little girl. It was love at first sight. We were married six months later and we stayed together for almost thirty years. And they were wonderful years, for us, the happiest I've ever been. We traveled together though we spent most of our time in South Africa. As you know, it was an international pariah, back then, and with good reason. We could have just left. We talked about it once or twice. But Victor was committed to making the country a better place and so was I. I had dabbled in philanthropy before but now... Victor and I saw so much. My only regret is that we couldn't do more... but I'm digressing," she said, interrupting herself.

"When your husband died..." Berté prompted.

"I began traveling again. I often go back to South Africa to see Christine and my grandchildren, but I'm no longer happy living in Cape Town. Too many memories."

"And so we finally come to the present."

Van Der Meer sighed. "Yes, I suppose we do." She paused, steeling herself. "I was supposed to be in that bed with Roberto, not Ornella."

"Yes." said Berté. "Your Argentine 'stepson' certainly thought so."

Van Der Meer blanched. "Yes, but... I don't... how did you..."

"You recognized him at the hotel didn't you? That's why you hired a bodyguard."

"Yes." She had regained her composure. "It had been fifty years since I had last seen him but that's not a face I'm likely to forget. It was a shock, but I did my best to feign indifference so I don't think he realizes that I know he's there. The moment I recognized him, I knew what must have happened and my first instinct was to flee. I came here first."

"But what I don't understand," said Berté, exasperated, "is why you didn't just come to me and have this man arrested."

"You might have… said no. I didn't know what evidence you had or leads you were pursuing. I come to you with a story about a child who killed puppies fifty years ago and what are you going to do? I couldn't even prove that this person is who I say he is. And I have no idea what he has been doing for the last half-century. For all I know, he's now a police officer himself. What if he had simply denied everything? What would you have done? 'Oh, sorry Sir. This woman claims she knew you in 1967 so we're locking you up for murder.'"

"Hmm. Yes. I see your point." admitted Berté.

"And what would he have done once I had accused him? No, Inspector, I couldn't take the risk."

"But you were going to take the risk. Monsignor Citterio said you had already planned to call me before I arrived."

She sighed again. "That's true. Monsignor Citterio reminded me that sometimes you have to do the right thing and leave the rest to God. I can't let a murderer — a murderer who killed my employees, my friends — escape justice no matter what it might cost me personally. I suppose I knew that already when I chose to come here because I knew what the monsignor would advise."

What followed was a succession of telephone calls. Berté called Parodi first with a long list of instructions. Next was the prosecutor, who was going to be equally busy. Finally, he called the chief of police and Gianasio. Berté tried to keep the calls brief but the prosecutor, in particular, insisted on pestering him for the details. In the end, Berté had to tell him the whole story. Grossi was particularly struck by Van Der Meer's ability to keep her true identity hidden for so many years. To Berté, that was the least remarkable aspect of the affair, but Grossi had the soul of an accountant.

The monsignor and his sister invited Berté and Van Der Meer to stay for lunch. But the countess had no appetite and Berté was in a hurry to get back to Lungariva so he made do with a light snack of *pizzette*, focaccia, and cheesecake which he ate standing up while Van Der Meer collected her luggage. Van Der Meer wanted to go back in her Bentley but Berté put his foot down. It wasn't that he didn't trust her, but he knew what would happen to him if he let her disappear again. So the bodyguard drove the Bentley back and the countess squeezed into his battered Lancia Delta. He wondered what she would make of that but she didn't seem to mind.

On the trip back to Lungariva, Berté contemplated his next move. Had this been a bad detective novel, he would have gathered everyone together in the library and gotten the murderer to confess. But criminals were seldom so obliging in real life.

Van Der Meer, too, remained silent and Berté wondered what was going on inside her head. For Berté, the scene that was about to play out at a hotel in Lungariva would wrap up a difficult four days. Van Der Meer had lived a lie for more than fifty years and it was all about to come crashing down.

Not to mention that she'll have to confront a murderer.

True. That was all in a day's work for Berté but civilians like Van Der Meer had more delicate sensibilities. This was going to be difficult. He carefully observed her out of the corner of his eye. She appeared tired, confused. For the first time since he had known her, she looked her age.

"I have to ask you a favor, Signora."

Van Der Meer continued to stare out the window. "Yes?" she said, almost mechanically.

Berté sighed. "I might need you to confront our murderer. Do you think you are up to it?"

The countess continued to stare at the highway. She was silent several seconds before saying, "If you must. Perhaps that is part of my penance."

When the white bulk of the Grand Hotel Miramare finally hove into view, Berté pulled to the side of the road. "We're going to go down into the parking garage," he told Van Der Meer. "I'll escort you directly up to your room where your bodyguard will be waiting.

Don't leave your room for any reason. This is my cell phone number, call me if you need me. If we need you, either myself or Detective Gianasio will come to get you. Don't open the door for anyone else."

Berté put the car back into drive, drove into the parking garage, and hustled Van Der Meer into the elevator. When the elevator door opened on her floor, a uniformed officer was waiting for them outside her room, with Consuelo and the bodyguard standing next to him. The countess gave Berté a weak smile and a nod before entering the room, followed by her bodyguard.

*****

The prosecutor and Gianasio were waiting for him in the usual room. He briefly summarized for them what he had in mind. The prosecutor stared at him silently for a few moments, then said, "You're sure the countess is telling the truth? That she's not lying in an attempt to derail the investigation?"

"An excellent point." Berté could be diplomatic when he had to. "I can't rule it out one hundred percent, which is why we need to hear the other side of the story. I'd like to start by speaking with our suspect alone."

"All right, do as you see fit," said Grossi as he exited, followed by Gianasio. "I'll wait in the next room in case you need me. And if you are right, you will."

"Then let's get started. Bring me Gomez." ordered Berté.

A few minutes later, an officer escorted Signor Fernando Luis Gomez, supermarket owner and Argentine importer of Italian products, into the room.

"Please sit down." said Berté, motioning to the chair in front of him.

"Inspector, this is the *tercera vez* that you've called me in to speak with you and that your officers have detained me. This treatment is outrageous. I called *mi amigo* from Rapallo, who is sending me a lawyer. He's calling my consulate as well."

"Please forgive me. We Italian police officers can be very excitable and annoying."

"You are ruining my vacation. What more do you want from me?"

"Just the truth. Nothing more."

"I've already told you the truth."

"Have you really? Are you still claiming that you have never met Signora Van Der Meer? But perhaps you are confused. Does the name Lucia d'Andrea refresh your memory?" Berté saw a flash of hatred in the man's eyes at the mention of Lucia d'Andrea. It only lasted for a second, but Berté knew he was right. Now all he had to do was get his quarry into the net.

But Signor Gomez was not yet ready to admit defeat. "You were *bien informado* and I can imagine *también* who told you this…" he said, shaking his head. "*Yo preferí* ignore her the moment that I saw her here in the hotel. It had been more than *cincuenta años…*" he said, looking down at the table.

"Continue."

"*Esto es muy difícil para mí!* I mean… It's not easy, you know? I was barely a kid when my father brought home this *callejera*."

"*Callejera?*"

"*Una copera de cabaret!* One of those women who dance with men in nightclubs… She arrived in Argentina poor and on the make. I don't know how…" Gomez paused. "But you know all this, at least her version."

"Why don't you tell me your version?" said Berté dryly. Gomez was using a mix of Spanish and Italian, which was testing both Berté's linguistic abilities and his patience.

"*Esa perra,* that bitch, she can seem like *un angel* but she is *una bruja,* a witch! She seduced *mi padre sólo* to rob us, *a él y a mi, un pibe de tan sólo 16 años…*""

"Please, speak in Italian! You know the language well!"

Fernando Gomez went silent, staring into the distance and into the past. "When my father, how do you say, *morir?*" he finally began, still staring at nothing. "It turned out she had taken everything. She left me with only what she couldn't sell, just *la estancia* itself and a few head of mangy cattle. Everything else had been sold off and she had run away with the *dinero*. Of course, I tried to find her but it was useless. It was as if Lucia d'Andrea had been swallowed by the earth. And now I know why." reflected Gomez bitterly. "For all I knew, she was dead until I saw her at breakfast in this hotel. At first, I could not believe my *ojos*."

Gomez suddenly stopped and fixed his gaze on Berté. "But these stories from my past are of no interest to you. Yes, I knew the woman you call Van Der Meer, though, *Dios mio,* I wish that I did not. But I never met your two murder victims. I don't even know their names."

Berté returned Fernando Gomez's gaze. "I agree. You did not. And that only makes it worse. I have my own theory about how things happened that night. Around 10pm, someone heard the bartender take a call from Countess Van Der Meer for an order of herbal tea to be delivered to room 422. At around 11:30, that same someone saw the bartender take a bottle of champagne and two glasses up to room 422. And, just like the bartender did, our someone assumed that Countess Van Der Meer was still in room 422 and would be there for quite some time. He made his way back to his room, loaded the gun that he had obtained on his 'walk', and visited room 422 himself at about midnight. The rest, as they say, is history."

"And you think I am 'someone'?" sneered Gomez. "I think we are done here. I have nothing more to say until my lawyer arrives." he said, crossing his arms and lowering his gaze.

Berté sighed and stood up. It was only to be expected. But it meant Berté would have to report to Grossi and that he would have to sit in on the interview when it continued. It was time to play his ace. Berté had just instructed Gianasio to bring down Van Der Meer when the lawyer sent by Gomez's friend arrived. He was a man in his sixties, with a permanently exasperated expression. He apparently knew the prosecutor and greeted him by name.

As they chatted, Berté once again examined his phone as if he could summon the message he had been waiting for by strength of will. To his considerable shock, it rang. But it was only Dr. Filippi, Brioschi's attending physician.

"Doctor Filippi, how's our patient?" asked Berté.

"Not so good," responded Filippi dryly. "He passed away a few minutes ago. I thought you'd want to know right away."

"Oh. I understand. Did he…"

"No, he never regained consciousness," said Filippi, anticipating his question. "I did tell you that his condition was serious."

"Yes. You did. Thank you for all your help, Doctor. I hope to meet you again under different circumstances."

"Same to you, Inspector."

Berté frowned. Another death. And for what? He couldn't be prosecuted for it, but Ferrari's killer had yet another life on his conscience.

The lawyer had gone into the room where Fernando Gomez was being held to confer privately with his client. After a few minutes, he opened the door and indicated they were ready. Berté wasn't, however. He was still waiting for Van Der Meer.

After about ten minutes, Gianasio entered the hallway and gestured to Berté. He nodded to Gianasio and entered the room where Gomez, his lawyer and Grossi, the prosecutor, had already gathered.

It's showtime. Hope you get good reviews.

Berté sat down and crossed his fingers. He was risking a lot on this. If that message he was waiting for never came, he would have to bluff. Van Der Meer was right. He couldn't lock Gomez up because he was an obnoxious teenager fifty years ago.

When Van Der Meer entered the room, Gomez froze, staring, his face a mixture of hatred and fear. Van Der Meer herself was imperturbable and as graceful as a dancer. She greeted Berté and Grossi courteously while ignoring Gomez… No, ignoring wasn't quite the right word. She was obviously aware that he was present but she treated him as if he were a disgusting insect that had somehow managed to crash a royal event. Her disdain was a physical force, dominating the room. Even Grossi noticed.

Berté could not hide his deep admiration for her *sang froid*. Sitting in front of him, she gave him a friendly, albeit tense, smile. He knew how hard this face-to-face confrontation must be for her but her self-control was immaculate. She never even glanced in the direction of Fernando Gomez. He, on the other hand, continued to stare at her, petrified. Perhaps this might work after all.

"So…" Berté began, clearing his throat as all eyes were focused on him, "Lucia D'Andrea, do you recognize Fernando Gomez as the son of the man that you lived with for six years in Argentina?"

"Yes."

"And do you, Fernando Gomez, recognize Lucia D'Andrea?"

Gomez remained silent for a moment. "This woman ruined my

life," he finally said in a strangled voice. "She deprived me of *el amor de mi padre* and stole *mi* inheritance!"

The fuse is lit, thought Berté, seeing the slightest of blushes creep up Van Der Meer's face.

"I stole nothing." said the countess, almost paternalistically, "your father did what he did of his own volition, not because of me, but because of you. And it was I who convinced him to leave you what he did leave you, the *estancia* where you had grown up."

"Bitch! You… you bewitched *mi padre*! From the moment you appeared, you cast some sort of spell on him. You took over his life and destroyed mine!" Gomez was shouting now.

The lawyer placed a hand on his arm to calm him and tried to intervene. "Deputy Assistant Chief," he said, looking at Berté questioningly, "I don't understand what you are getting at… Are you not investigating the deaths of this lady's two employees? Or do you have some sort of special jurisdiction from the government of Argentina to investigate the theft of my client's patrimony?"

"Be patient, counselor, all things come to those who wait," said Berté somewhat rudely. "For the moment, we are simply establishing some relevant facts."

"You're lying, Inspector!" Gomez blurted out. "You have already accused me of killing these people that I have never met because *esta ratera* says so."

"The years have taught you nothing. You are still your own worst enemy." taunted the countess with a superior smile.

"Liar! *Puta!*"

"Watch your language, Signor Gomez," warned the prosecutor, who didn't understand Spanish but had no trouble interpreting Gomez's obvious rage.

"None of you know her! You don't know what she is or what she's capable of! *Transformó a mi padre* into her slave! In the end, she killed him!"

"You're pathetic, Fernando. I pity you. I pitied you then and I pity you now," Van Der Meer declared.

"Enough. Silence!" Grossi commanded. "And you, Berté, get to the point."

Berté's phone began to vibrate. A quick glance revealed an incoming call from Parodi. "Excuse me, I need to take this," said

Berté, ignoring Grossi's scandalized expression. "And?" he asked, without preamble.

"We found them. It was just as you thought."

Berté hung up without further comment and turned his attention to Gomez.

"Now, Signor Gomez, "you claim that on the night of the murder, you left the bar and went back to your room at about 11:30 and that you did not leave your room again until you came down the next morning. Is that correct?"

"*Claro que sí*! I don't just 'claim' it. It's true!"

"But it's not true, is it? You were in the bar when you heard tea being sent up to room 422 for Countess Van Der Meer. You were also in the bar at 11:30 when a bottle of champagne and two glasses were sent up to room 422. This must have seemed like the perfect moment to take the revenge you had been planning for the last two days. Not only would you finally kill the woman you believe had ruined your life, you would ensure that she would be remembered, not as a beloved philanthropist, but as a figure of mockery and scandal. So you went up to your room, loaded your gun, put the master key you had stolen in your pocket, and waited until well after midnight when you could be sure you would encounter no one in the hallways and elevators. Then you made your way to room 422, unlocked the door, and emptied your gun into the two figures in the bed. But you did not know that Van Der Meer was no longer in room 422 and that Signora Ferrari had taken her place. My greatest regret in this case is that I did not see your face the next morning when your 'victim' turned up and ordered breakfast."

Gomez was shaking now, whether in fear or in fury, Berté couldn't tell. After making a physical effort to master himself, he turned to his lawyer, almost shouting. "Have you nothing to say? He's accusing me of murder! Are you just going to sit there while this *cabron* invents fairy tales?"

Gomez's lawyer again put a hand on his client's arm. "Signor Gomez is understandably upset. But he does have a point. From what I can tell, this is all the product of Deputy Assistant Chief Berté's excellent imagination. It's speculation, and extravagant speculation at that. If that is your case against my client, I think we will be going now. You have no actual evidence at all."

"Well, your client has repeatedly lied to the police during this investigation. That is, of course, suspicious. But it's also a crime in itself. So your client is not going anywhere at the moment. And as for evidence, your client left the hotel the morning after the murder at 8:40 carrying a bag. He did not return until 10:00."

"And that is your evidence?" The lawyer smiled. "My client regularly attends Mass in the mornings. Or do you imagine that he went to confession instead?"

Berté was beginning to enjoy himself. "Perhaps he did. But he also dropped off a bundle of clothes in the Caritas bin for the poor. We found them this afternoon. It was quite a nice suit with an Argentine label. And before your client says anything, one of the pockets had a bar receipt with his name on it. You must be more careful next time, Signor Gomez."

A bead of perspiration ran down Gomez's forehead and he angrily wiped it away. "I am a religious man. I often donate to the poor. The bin was full of clothing donated by dozens of people. Do you accuse them of murder as well? This means nothing!"

"Your piety does you credit." said Berté dryly. "But your donation was special, truly unique. That call I just received was the lab results confirming that the clothes you donated were covered with gunpowder residue. You were wearing that suit when you gunned down Signora Ferrari and Signor Sommariva." Berté turned to Gomez's lawyer. "Is that enough evidence for you?" he asked politely.

Gomez's face was frozen in a rictus of hatred while the lawyer's was frozen in an expression of resignation. A heavy silence reigned. It was Van Der Meer who broke the spell.

"You are just as much of an embarrassment now as you were then. You have learned nothing in fifty years." She said this without sarcasm and without rancor, as if she were commenting on the weather.

Gomez snapped. With a snarl, he launched himself toward the countess, arms outstretched, and with murder in his eyes… only to be met by Berté's waiting fist.

The entire room was frozen in shock, except for Gomez who, his momentum suddenly reversed, landed back in his seat, nose bloodied and eyes glazed. Gianasio pirouetted out of her chair and neatly handcuffed his limp arms behind his back. Berté had warned her to expect something like this.

"Am I correct in assuming that this is no longer an interview pursuant to Article 351 of the Code of Criminal Procedure and that the provisions of the second and third sentences of paragraph 1 of Article 362 no longer apply?" asked Gomez's lawyer courteously.

Berté was still shaking his hand in pain and swearing under his breath – punching someone always looked so much easier in the movies – when Gomez began shouting. "*Puta de mierda!* You are my ruin! Why didn't you die in that room? Go to hell. But even the devil won't have you!"

He began to cry like a child. An old child, thought Berté, who had never really grown up. Berté hated Gomez for what he had done. But he could not help wondering if this was Van Der Meer's fault after all. If she had made different choices… if his father had made different choices, all those years ago, perhaps things might have been different, and three innocent people might still be alive.

For all sad words of tongue or pen, the saddest are these: It might have been.

Grossi, still rattled, decided to reassert himself. "That's enough, Signor Gomez! Take him away and book him."

Gianasio led the still-sobbing Gomez from the room while Grossi moved to where Van Der Meer was still sitting, unruffled. Grossi, usually never at a loss for words, began to stammer. "Later, I will have to... You understand… Those identity papers. I will have to inform the authorities in Pordenone."

"Yes, of course, you do. Do what you have to," the countess murmured. "In any case, the name 'Licia' no longer serves me now..." She stood up, smiled at the prosecutor and nodded in dismissal. Turning to Berté, she said. "Thank you."

"There is no need," said Berté with a slight smile. "I was fulfilling a solemn promise I had made."

"To God?"

"Much more solemn than that, Countess. To Monsignor Citterio."

Van Der Meer looked at him, surprised. "You called me countess! You've never done that, before!" her periwinkle eyes twinkled ironically. "I had to earn my title in the field, apparently."

"With distinction!" laughed Berté.

"Thank you again, Inspector." At the door, Countess Van Der

Meer turned back. "And put some ice on that hand!"

Now Berté had to endure an outpouring of gratitude and praise from Grossi. "Endure" was the right word. Berté did not enjoy being the center of attention even under normal conditions. And when a case had finally concluded – especially this case – he needed time on his own to process everything.

Grossi, however, was just the beginning. Before long, the chief of police, Roberto Terani, was on the phone congratulating him and wanting to hear all the details directly from Berté's lips. Berté was flattered, even though he knew that Terani would be relaying those details directly to the press as soon as Berté hung up the phone.

Better him than you.

Berté couldn't have agreed more. He was already getting much more attention than he wanted. Even Gianasio wanted to shake Berté's hand. Fortunately, he stopped her just in time and got her to bring him the ice the countess had recommended instead.

But when Garaventa, the hotel manager, turned up and began gushing his thanks, it was too much. Here, finally, was someone Berté could safely ignore.

"Oh, Inspector, I can't thank you enough! You must sit down with me and tell me the whole story…"

"I'm sorry but I'm very…" Berté began to interrupt.

"…over dinner."

"… hungry!" finished Berté, quickly changing course.

Once again, the Grand Hotel Miramare did not disappoint. First came the usual focaccia pyramid. Tonight, the chef sent up two first courses, Shrimp Portofino followed by house-made ravioli filled with potato and pesto, in a sauce of melted butter and string beans. Both courses were accompanied by a chilled bottle of Vermentino Colli di Luni to wash them down. For dessert, there was a lemon tart made with cocoa shortbread pastry. To finish, Berté had a double espresso. He still had to make it home, after all.

It's a pity there isn't a murder in the Grand Hotel every week.

Berté, of course, didn't agree. But he had to admit this was a far more enjoyable place to investigate a murder than some seedy alleyway.

Parodi turned up just as Berté was finishing his excellent meal. Garaventa took his leave, thanking Berté profusely. Parodi looked at him oddly, unaware that Berté had privately assured him over dinner that his unfortunate indiscretion with Ornella Ferrari need go no further.

"What's wrong with your hand?" asked Parodi curiously as he sat down at the table. Berté gave his sergeant a full report of the evening's events, complete with color commentary. Parodi was suitably impressed. "When you ordered us to start searching charity bins, I thought you were just desperate. But you were right again."

Ligurians, thought Berté, were the English of Italy, undemonstrative to a fault. But he knew that for Parodi, this was high praise and it meant more to him that Grossi's flowery congratulations.

"And we didn't need *them*." by which Parodi meant the contingent from Genoa.

Berté smiled. "Come on, Pasquale! Don't be like that. They were very helpful! Think of all the leg work they saved us. Did you want to interview a hundred hotel guests by yourself? It's all grist to the mill. It's been a long four days. Go home and get some rest. Gomez is in custody and the rest of the paperwork can wait until tomorrow."

"Thank you for your gracious kindness most noble Sir. If you will forgive my impertinence, go home and get some rest yourself!"

"Am I uglier than usual?" joked Berté.

"Well, your ponytail *is* a bit limp. And put some ice on that hand!"

Berté jokingly started to hit him with a quick jab and then thought better of it. He really should have that hand looked at! He still had one call to make. In a way, it was really Belli who had cracked the case.

He finished his call with Belli and made his way to the lobby where he ran into Sabatini who offered to drive him home. Berté smiled. He'd never before worked with people as devoted and as… considerate as his little team. In Milan, he had worked with some people who would not have picked him up if he had been run over in the street. That was yet another plus to working in Lungariva. "I appreciate the offer, Sabatini. But I feel like walking." said Berté. "You go on home yourself. You did excellent work on this case. Thank you."

"It's kind of you to say so. And Sir?"

"Yes?"

"You really should put some ice on that hand."

*****

Berté made his way through town, his collar up against the cold, humid air. Was this the warm, Mediterranean climate of the Riviera they always touted in the travel brochures? He couldn't remember the last time he'd been this cold.

Really? You can't remember the last time you were in Milan? This is nothing!

The Bastard had a point. He was forgetting all the things he'd really hated about Milan and focusing, instead, on all the things he mildly disliked in Lungariva. On top of that he was… not depressed, exactly. But when he concluded a case, especially one as involved as this one, there was always a sense of emptiness, a feeling that he was at loose ends. It was only natural, he supposed, but it was disconcerting to think that he only felt truly alive when investigating a murder, like a sort of criminological vampire.

Berté shook himself. This wouldn't do. The real reason, he thought grimly, that he was so wrapped up in his work was that it allowed him to ignore what passed for his personal life. Should he stay in Lungariva or go back to Milan? Should he patch things up with Marzia or go back to Patty? As long as he had a fresh corpse to hand, he didn't have to deal with any of that. Well, no more. He had decided. He was going to get his personal life in order and the first step was fixing things with Marzia. After that, he'd see. It was all a matter of having the right attitude. He was not a victim and the Universe was not conspiring against him.

He approached the Pensione Aurora with a new determination in his stride. When he entered the lobby, he could see a light in the office behind the reception desk. So Marzia was in and there was no time like the present. He walked up and rang the bell.

"Yes? Oh, it's you! How's the investigation going?"

"Successfully concluded."

"That's fantastic! You're… Oh my God! What did you do to your hand? Let me get you some ice for that!"

"Yes, it's pretty sore. That would be… No! No! Forget the ice! Marzia, I…" Berté's little speech was interrupted by the ringing of the office phone.

"Just a minute, Luigi, I'd better get that… Pensione Aurora, may I help you? Yes, Signora. Your boyfriend? Oh, really? Indeed. Can you just hold for a moment? Thank you."

Marzia turned to Berté, smiling dangerously. "It's a Signora Patty Astesani. She heard on the radio that you've solved the case, so she's coming down to celebrate with you. Isn't that nice!" said Marzia, handing him the phone.

Somewhere, in the distance, Berté could hear the Universe laughing.

The End

If you enjoyed this book, please leave us an online review, even if it's just a star rating. Your opinion will influence thousands of readers and we really appreciate your feedback!